Newfoundland
Pony Tales

Andrew F. Fraser

Illustrations by
Cliff George

Edited by
Trudy J. Morgan-Cole

Newfoundland
Pony Tales

Andrew F. Fraser

Illustrations by
Cliff George

Edited by
Trudy J. Morgan-Cole

Tuckamore Books
St. John's, Newfoundland
1996

We acknowledge the support of The Canada Council for the Arts for our publishing program.

∞ Printed on acid-free paper

Published by

CREATIVE BOOK PUBLISHING
a division of 10366 Newfoundland Limited
a Robinson-Blackmore Printing & Publishing associated company
P.O. Box 8660, St. John's, Newfoundland A1B 3T7

First printing March 1996
Second Printing June 1999

Printed in Canada by:
ROBINSON-BLACKMORE PRINTING & PUBLISHING

Canadian Cataloguing in Publication Data

Fraser, Andrew F. (Andrew Ferguson)

 Newfoundland pony tales

 ISBN 1-895387-67-1

1. Newfoundland pony — Juvenile fiction   I. George, Cliff.
II. Morgan-Cole, Trudy J.   III. Title

SF315.2.N48F47 1996   j636.1609718   C96-950040-8

To the Newfoundland Ponies
and those who raised and nurtured them

The stories in this book are based on true events.
To protect privacy some names have been altered,
but all the people and ponies are real characters.

Contents

Preface: A Look Back

This is a book of stories about Newfoundland Ponies. What is a Newfoundland Pony? To understand the answer to that question, we need to take a look back in history, to understand where this pony came from and the part it plays in our province's history and heritage.

For much of human history, horses have been an important part of human life. That is no longer true as it once was, yet people still feel a bond to horses and an admiration for the vital role they once played. Horse-power was used in many ways, mostly for transport and work. In the attempts to cultivate the earth, even to survive, mankind would have had little success without this animal.

The ancient Celtic people were the most important horse-based culture in European history. Celts not only used but even worshipped their Celtic ponies. As the Celts moved from central Europe, westwards into Brittany in France, then across the sea to England and beyond to Wales, Ireland, and the western coastline of Scotland, they left their culture in every region they colonised. The Celts were well established in Britain long before the Roman arrival in 54 B.C.

According to the writings of Caesar, Celts were warriors who used horses with skill. In these writings the Celts were described as high-spirited, frank, with a keen sense of honour but warlike, and much given to religion, philosophy and poetry. Archeological findings have shown that the Celtic people built stone buildings using the power of horses, for their culture did not have slave labour. Among such Celtic artifacts as decorated pots, weaving combs, wooden writing tablets, metal writing instruments, leather tents, tools for carpentry, and farming tools, archeologists have also found items for horse-shoeing, harnessing, and wooden carriage wheels. Clearly these people were not only a cultured and organized race but they were people who used horses and horse power.

The type of horse the Celts had brought with them through Europe was called *Equus Celticus*; it had evolved in the northern part of Europe during the Ice Age and was well adapted to life in colder climates. Whatever horses were already in Britain before the Celts came had probably bred with the Celtic ponies, so that by the time the Romans came to Britain, *Equus Celticus* was the most common breed of horse in Britain. We know little about Equus Celticus, except that Caesar described it as a hardy pony of a compact type. This useful Celtic pony became an ancestor of the various types of native ponies that later emerged in the British Islands.

While *Equus Celticus* was evolving during the Ice Age, some other strains of horses, not so well adapted to the cold, moved south to the Mediterranean lands. They became the ancestors of the Arabian horse. Domestic horses are often divided into "cold-blood" and "warm-blood" types, but this view does not give a complete picture, because ponies do not fit neatly into either of these categories.

Heavy draft horses like Clydesdales are called "cold-blooded" because of they are passive in nature and move slowly. Cold-blooded horses have thick heavy bodies and strong legs. The head has a broad nose and flattish face, with nostrils which are tight - not flared open. On some, heavy hair drapes the lower parts of the leg and hangs over the hooves and heels. In others, with smaller hooves, prominent tufts of hair project from the back of the legs. Cold-blooded horses are strong and unemotional, not high-spirited.

Warm blooded horses, such as the Thoroughbred and the Arabian, are considered to be spirited and temperamental. They can also be self-willed. They look different too, with a flat or concave face, out-reached neck, long slender limbs and a tail of high carriage. They have a "hot-blooded" image compared to their distant northern cousins. There is really no difference in the blood of the two types of horses, but in spirit, temperament, and physique, they are quite different.

But where do ponies fit in? In terms of "spirit," ponies lie somewhere between "warm" and "cold." They can be classed as "cool-blooded," but they do not have the enormous bulk of true cold-blooded horses. Furthermore, ponies have brighter disposition and more "character" in their temperament. Really , all the pony has in common with the great heavyweight horses is its hardiness. The pony is truly in a class by itself.

We have seen that the first pure pony was the ancient Celtic pony. This is the distant ancestor of our own Newfoundland Pony. The native pack horses of the British Isles were direct descendants of the Celtic Pony. They were the work horses—the "beasts of burden"—for the rural British and Irish people. When the pioneers, such as John Guy, came to Newfoundland this was the type of work horse they brought with them. These small horses took to this island as well as they had taken to all the British Islands in prehistoric times.

The ships that made the first journeys across the Atlantic were small, with sail power alone to make the rough crossing. This made it difficult to transport a large number of farm animals. If the colonists were to have livestock in their new home, the animals they brought over would have to be carefully preserved so that they could reproduce. The farm animals were essential for settlement and Newfoundland's pioneers knew this.

Nobody knows for sure when the first settlement took place in Newfoundland, but it is believed that by 1522, twenty-five years after Cabot's discovery of Newfoundland, there were about fifty dwelling houses here. These were the homes of fishermen who did not return to England at the end of the fishing season but spent the winter here. In the early 1600s, a businessman named John Guy in the city of Bristol, England, decided to organize an expedition to go and settle this New Found Land. In 1610 Guy sailed with three ships and 41 people, and anchored at Cupids in Conception Bay. His expedition brought "goats, swine, cows and poultry." It is believed that Guy also brought horses on this first voyage. When he saw the settlement nicely established, John Guy went back to England to report and to get more supplies for his plantation experiment on the island. Along with more people, cattle, pigs and poultry, Guy brought more horses.

The horses Guy brought in the early 1600's were probably the first horses in Newfoundland. Nobody has described what kind of horses these were, but they were probably the Exmoor and Dartmoor ponies native to the region Guy sailed from.

After John Guy gave up his venture and left Newfoundland, some of his people stayed behind, along with their animals. In the years that followed, other Englishmen made attempts to settle Newfoundland, like Lord Falkland, who arrived in Newfoundland and ordered a further supply of horses to be shipped from Bristol. He specified horses of both sexes, for breeding, and he indicated the need for horses of the "hardy type that can live on hard ground." His instructions were that such horses could be obtained in parts of Scotland, Ireland and Wales. In due course Lord Falkland got his horses and he established his colony at Renews. Falkland, like Guy before him, left after a few years, but his animals were left behind, and since they were hardy animals, they probably survived.

After that, people were discouraged from settling in Newfoundland for many years, and so there was no great increase in the numbers of either people or livestock for nearly two hundred years. But when settlement became encouraged again in the early 1800's, the cultivation of the land was once again important and the horse came back into the picture. For hauling logs from the woods the horse was essential. This timber was needed for the building of boats, wharfs, flakes, houses and other buildings vital to the fishing industry.

More horses, usually small draft horses, came from Britain. Horses were brought as well from New England and Nova Scotia. All of these bred with the ponies that were already on the island, and a very well-mixed pony population resulted. The total number of ponies and horses in Newfoundland was 1,551 by 1836. Nine years later the figure was 2,409. By 1847 the population of horses numbered over four thousand. Most of these were in Conception Bay.

By this time, a population of wild ponies had become established on Sable Island. The true origin of these ponies is uncertain, but some of them were brought to Newfoundland. A record from September, 1852 tells of a ship called the *Maria* which "sailed for Newfoundland having forty horses and sufficient quantity of hay in board." (Information supplied by Mrs. Barbara Christie of the Nova Scotia Museum). We do not know for sure where these forty ponies ended up, but many of them probably were dropped off at Marystown. There would have been mares, stallions, colts, fillies and foals in this shipment, and since it was September, many of the mares would have been pregnant. In 1911, the Morris government of Newfoundland imported another shipload of Sable Island ponies to invigorate the local breed. Thus some of the Sable Island ponies became part of the Newfoundland Pony breed.

The number of horses in Newfoundland grew steadily during all of the nineteenth century and by 1901 there were 8,851 counted on the official census. By 1921 there was total of 16,340 horses of all kinds. In 1935 the government of Newfoundland first made a distinction between horses and ponies in the official records. In that year the census gave the figures of 5,658 horses and 9,025 ponies. The Newfoundland Pony was a provincial fact that was evident in its great population. Within two years, by 1938, the pony population must have touched 10,000. Another breed was then added, two dozen Welsh ponies that arrived from Toronto in 1939 and were cross-bred with the Newfoundland Pony. At its peak, sometime after the Second World War, the population of Newfoundland Ponies has been roughly estimated at twelve thousand.

The Newfoundland Pony, then, grew as a breed just as Newfoundlanders grew into a distinct people. They supported and established each other. The pony and its people travelled the same route until machines drove them apart.

The Newfoundland Pony was highly regarded for its durability, its long life, and its sociable nature. It was a variable breed and there was a pony for every need. Some were fairly large — around 900 pounds, others were neat and small — around 500 pounds; most were about 700 pounds in weight and 12.2 hands in height. All these ponies thrived well in Newfoundland's climate; their thick coats were ideal for North Atlantic winters and their mixed backgrounds gave them strength and vigour.

Some of these horses had a good trotting gait while some were better at steady, slow work. Their colours varied but mostly they were a dark bay colour. Black manes, tails and legs were usual but the body colour could be black, brown, reddish, grey or roan. Some of the roans, with their white hairs finely intermingled with darker hairs, had a bluish or strawberry hue. The roans and some of solid colours even changed their shade with seasons, being light in colour in the summer and very dark in winter. Pinto colouring and white legs were not typical colour characteristics, but some had a white foot or two.

Nobody made any great effort to keep track of breeding. Foals were born each summer and usually no-one knew who the sire was. It was not considered important for ponies to have papers. Each young pony's identity was simply based on what was evident, its appearance and its mother's reputation. Ponies were seldom high-priced because they were numerous and also because they were more often traded for some other necessity or given away as a favour.

Some people believed that it was important for the Newfoundland Pony to be officially recognized as a breed, but this never happened, although it was a member in its own right of the ancient family of Mountain and Moorland ponies that became classified into nine modern breeds in England, Scotland, Wales and Ireland at the start of the twentieth century.

The arrival of machines to do much of the work that horses once did changed the story of the Newfoundland Pony, and its numbers began to decline. Pony numbers have been falling fast since 1978, when the horse meat trade first focused on this animal. But there were still about three or four thousand left when the Animal Pedigree Act came into effect in 1988. At that time, if people had been sufficiently aware, the Newfoundland Pony could have been given the status of an official breed. But this did not happen, although some people in the Newfoundland Pony Society tried to present a case. The opportunity has passed. The pony was left out of Canada's recognized breeds, and its numbers dwindled dangerously fast, 'til it almost became extinct. Today it is reduced to a breeding population of less than one hundred.

Some of the remaining ponies need friendship more than bureaucracy. They need food and care more than documentation. They need charity more than paper status. For these reasons a group of concerned people have collaborated under the name *Friends of the Newfoundland Pony*. There are now about forty "Friends" dealing with thirty-two ponies. A "Friend" is simply anyone who helps in the care of the ponies by donating time, attention or funds in order to provide good care for ponies in need. With such help the pony may have a future. The trend to extinction may have been halted.

In this project I am joined by Cliff George, the popular artist in this province. Cliff has illustrated each chapter with lifelike sketches. He knows many of the ponies that are in these stories. Cliff and I have been partners in many Newfoundland Pony projects and I am especially grateful to him for his strong support in this one.

All the stories in this book are based on true events. Some names and details have been altered to protect privacy, but all the people and ponies are real characters. I hope that these stories will reveal the worthiness of this animal and show its link with the people who cared for it in the past. The comparatively few ponies that remain in Newfoundland are still very deserving animals. Fortunately, they have the support of many people who are enduring friends of this horse, now recognized by government and society as this province's "Heritage Animal."

1 Cloudy

The old man, his eyes glinting with what might have been a spark of mischief, led the colt out of his stall into the weak October sunshine. "I think you'll find this is just the fellow you're looking for, Dr. Fraser," he said.

I had come to the old man's farm by the shore of Witless Bay looking for a Newfoundland colt to buy. Of course I intended to shop around—have a look at the old man's colt, then go see another colt I'd heard of so I could compare them. This was too important a purchase for me to make a sudden decision. But the young pony had other ideas. From the moment I saw him, he adopted me as his friend. I had no choice.

I had already been introduced to the colt's mother, a friendly little black mare. Now, as her colt walked across the yard toward me, I sensed his strong personality at once. He had a well-built body, an attractive face, firm legs, a compact neck and a twinkle in his eye. As I approached him, he came towards me. I fondled his head, and he pushed closer to me and laid his face against my stomach.

The old farmer grinned. "He's taken a liking to you," he said, nodding.

I'd taken a liking to him too, but I didn't want to tell his owner that right away. "What have you called him?" I asked.

"Prince," the old man replied.

1

I had already noticed that Newfoundland farmers seemed to call every male horse Prince and every female horse Queen, but in this case it was a good name for the little pony, who stood so regal in his bearing. His coat was almost black, with a fine grey tinge that gave him the colour of iron. He stood his ground calmly and looked up at me with his calm black eyes as I tried to bargain with his owner for a good price. The old man named a high price, but I knew it was no use to pretend I wasn't interested. It may have been foolish, but I paid twice the price for Prince that I'd planned on spending for a colt.

Yet as I led him away from his home, I thought I had still struck a good bargain. The colt's friendliness and confidence were obvious. He was a fine looking little fellow, iron-grey with a broad white ring around his right hind foot right up to his fetlock, a broad muzzle, and short ears tightly filled with furry hair. He stood only as high as my stomach, but I already knew he was going to play a big part in my life.

My first job as Prince's owner was to find a place for him to stay, so I went to see Mr. McNiven, who owned a big, old-fashioned horse barn on the road to Torbay. Mr. McNiven was a quiet, elderly man. I remember thinking he was very reserved when I first met him, but that was before we got talking about horses. He was one of the old style of work-horse men, and could talk for hours about horses and the old horse days. In fact, it sometimes seemed as though he liked horses more than people.

"So you've got yourself a colt, have you?" he said when I went to ask him about boarding Prince. "What d'you intend to do with him?"

"I'm very interested in Newfoundland Ponies, as you know," I told him, "and I've been on the lookout for a colt.

When he's older, I'll use him for breeding. He's a grand little pony, Mr. McNiven, wait till you see him."

Mr. McNiven only grunted. "Winter's coming on," he said, leading me into his barn, "and I'm about full already in here. Riding horses mostly—people in the city own 'em and board 'em up here." I followed him between the stalls, which were indeed full of big, fine-looking riding horses. It looked like there would be no room here for Prince.

We reached a corner of the barn that was piled high with odds and ends. Mr. McNiven looked at it, saying nothing for a moment. "I could probably clear this lot away," he said after a while. "There's a floorboard broken—" he kicked at it with his foot, "—and I'd need to repair that and put in a gate and a manger, and we'd have a stall for your pony. Would that be big enough?"

I looked at the little corner and imagined it a clean, well-kept stall like the others I had seen in Mr. McNiven's barn. This would certainly be a good home for Prince.

Mr. McNiven was a man of his word. In a few days, Prince's stall was ready and he moved in, travelling up the shore in the back of a pick-up truck. I wondered if he would miss his old home and his mother. But he was so interested in all the new things to see that he didn't seem to mind at all. In the big barn he had lots of other horses for company and plenty of attention from kind Mr. McNiven, who took to him just as quickly as I had done.

Prince quickly settled into his new life with Mr. McNiven. In the morning, his stall was shovelled out and freshly bedded with wood shavings. His water bucket was filled with fresh water from the hand pump in the barn. He got a flake of hay placed in a corner of his cosy stall. A jug of horse feed was emptied into his manger.

In the afternoon, Prince got another visit. Then he was turned outdoors into a nearby paddock. Here, along with one or two of the big riding horses who became his friends, Prince could romp and run freely. He could also look over the fence and see any excitement passing by, which often included planes taking off from the airport only a mile away. If the weather was fine, Prince stayed outside until dusk.

In the evenings, I came up to Mr. McNiven's barn to visit Prince. After I gave him hay and feed, filled his water bucket and tidied his stall, I got down to the job of grooming him. Each evening I brushed and combed him from head to hoof. This was Prince's favourite part of the day, as well as mine. He didn't mind if I picked up his hooves and cleaned his soles. He even put up with having knots tugged out of his mane and tail. But what he really loved was the body brushing.

Mr. McNiven noticed this one evening as he paused by Prince's stall and watched me groom my pony. "He likes that, doesn't he?" the horse man said. "A good horse always does."

I ran the brush over Prince's back and down his neck. "Makes him feel safe and cared-for," I observed.

"Not ticklish there, is he?" Mr. McNiven said as I brushed Prince's flank.

"No, though I've known horses who were," I said. "Some horses won't let you touch their flanks."

"Some horses don't like being groomed at all," said Mr. McNiven. "Bad-tempered ones, like that one over there," he nodded towards one of the riding horses at the far end of the barn, "can't abide being touched. But this one here loves it."

Prince stood quietly. His stillness, his flickering eyes, his relaxed mouth and the press of his head against my arm all told me how much he enjoyed our time together.

With fresh bedding again, Prince was ready for the night. Mr. McNiven, who had been tending to one of the other horses, waited for me and we left the barn together. As we closed the door, we heard, as I often did on these evenings, one or two subdued horse calls from the barn. "I wonder," I said to Mr. McNiven, "are they saying good night, or come again, or don't leave, or thanks for the visit?"

The older man was silent, and for a moment I thought he might think me foolish for having such fanciful notions about horses. But after a pause he said, "Us humans, Dr. Fraser, are not as smart as we think we are."

"That's for sure."

"Look at animals, now. We're supposed to be so much smarter than them, but we hardly understand them at all. I've worked with horses most of my life, and I still don't know half of what there is to know about them."

I pondered his words as night after night I said good-bye to Prince in his stall. It takes a long time to get to know even one animal very well. How much more difficult it is to understand animals in general! Horses have fears, wants, fondnesses and feelings, just as we do. The can be angry or pleased, afraid or friendly, compliant or resistant, in pain or at peace, active or tired. I believe they have many other feelings too. Delight and depression, fondness and hate, excitement and loneliness. Prince had feelings too. Some, like his fondness for me when I brushed him, were obvious from the moment we met. Others, I did not discover until my pony was much older and more mature.

My younger daughter, Sheila, had just finished high school in Saskatchewan and she came to live with me for six months before she went on to college in Scotland. She had always been a lover of animals; she had owned a stubborn little Shetland pony when she was a child. Sheila joined me in the routine visits to Prince each evening and soon saw how fond I was of this Newfoundland Pony. She did her share of the work in her jeans and heavy boots, helping to care for the pony. She took lots of photos of him—especially when he was changing colour between spring and summer.

"Dad," said Sheila when she was coming to the end of her stay, "I'm glad you're going to have such a special friend as this pony when I leave here to go to college. I'll be thinking of both of you. Let me know about the pony's progress, his schooling."

"Yes, Sheila," I said, "I'll make sure our horse gets some training."

"I suppose we all need our education," said Sheila with a smile and a sigh.

Throughout the summer and fall, I spent a lot of time outdoors with my yearling colt. I taught him to walk with me on a leading rein. He learned how to graze while tied to a rope tether. He also learned to stop and start and to back up on command. He learned to accept a bit in his mouth and to wear a saddle. I wanted him to grow to be a useful and manageable animal. At one year of age, Prince was showing his masculinity in his shape and strength. His neck and shoulders were becoming more developed. He was growing up fast to become a stallion. I kept Sheila well informed about all this.

Throughout that summer and fall, I spent as much time as I could with Prince. One day my friend Cliff, the artist, who was watching as I worked with Prince said, "You know, Andrew, I think Prince needs a longer name. It's time we started calling him Prince Andrew, because you and that pony are the best of friends!"

I laughed at that, but the name caught on and soon the pony's nickname became "Prince Andrew," often shortened to Drew. I didn't mind the name change, and the pony didn't seem to either. Changing a horse's name is no big deal—horses don't pay as much attention to their names as dogs do, for example. But I'd often thought that the name "Prince" wasn't really special enough for this pony. There were so many stallions called "Prince." And "Drew" sounded a bit too casual for such a fine animal, though as that summer and fall went on everyone began calling him by the new name.

As Drew's second winter arrived, we fell into the same routines we had followed the first winter. There were some changes. Mr. McNiven had fewer big horses in the barn this winter, and Drew got the biggest stall. I wondered at first why there weren't as many horses on Mr. McNiven's place this year, but as the winter went by and I visited with Mr. McNiven, I guessed the reason. Drew's caretaker moved more slowly now as he worked with his horses, and often stopped to rest while feeding a horse or cleaning out his stall. I began to realize that this old gentleman, who had done so much for my pony and for me, was no longer able to deal with all the chores that make up horse keeping. Of course kindly Mr. McNiven would never come out and say that taking care of Drew was too much of a burden for him, but I could sense it. When winter ended, I would have to find another place for Drew.

One fine day in spring, Mr. McNiven and I watched as Drew cantered around the paddock. Drew had shed his dark grey coat and acquired a beautiful light grey colour, which blended in with his dark coloured legs, dusky coloured head, and black mane and tail. His mane, which had never been cut, flowed out behind him when he ran, like the feathered headdress of an Indian chief.

"Well, he's grown up into a fine young stallion," Mr. McNiven said. "I could always see he would be, from the first day you brought him in here."

Drew, as if knowing we were complimenting him, tossed his fine head on his thick, strong neck and responded with a few loud neighs and vigorous snorts.

"He is indeed," I agreed, "and it's time to find a new home for him. You've been so kind," I added quickly, "but now that Prince is a stallion, he needs company."

"Mares' company!" agreed Mr. McNiven, nodding.

It was true. What Drew, as a healthy, vigorous young stallion, needed was the company of breeding mares. And a breeding herd of Newfoundland Ponies would be an excellent idea—especially if the ponies could be in a public location where people would have the opportunity to see them. I explained to Mr. McNiven the plan that had been developed.

"The Pippy Park Commission has agreed to fence off seventeen acres from Mount Scio Road down to Long Pond," I told him. This would run right past the building that was, at that time, the Premier's official residence. "It will be a pony sanctuary—for Drew and three mares. There'll be good grass land, plenty of woods, and lots of water."

The pony sanctuary was Drew's home for a year. In many ways, it was pony heaven. Drew enjoyed the beautiful grazing land and the company of his herd of mares. And he proved to be a good breeding stallion too, for the following spring, Drew's foals were born.

But one thing Drew didn't seem to enjoy was all the attention from the public. Although he had always liked people, I noticed when I went to visit him that his personality seemed to have changed a little. As master of his herd, he had become more aggressive. Though he was still his friendly self to me and to others he knew well, he was not the same around strangers—and there were lots of strangers! People often came to look over the fence at the little herd of Newfoundland Ponies and sometimes walked among them. Perhaps Drew felt he had to protect his mares and his foals from these intruders. I was sorry, but not really surprised, when one day I got a phone call saying that Drew had bitten a visitor to the park.

I hoped it wouldn't happen again, but it did. Finally I received the call I'd been dreading. "Drew is a danger to the public, Dr. Fraser," the voice on the other end of the line told me. He bit a woman who came to look at the ponies today. We can't keep him in Pippy Park any longer."

My heart was heavy as I went to bring Drew back from the pony sanctuary. No doubt he would miss his comfortable surroundings and his family of mares and foals. He stomped his hooves and neighed in protest as I led him away from the herd. I looked into the black eyes I had come to know so well and stroked his neck.

"Don't worry, old fellow," I told him. "I don't know what's going to become of you, but I'll take care of you, just as I always have."

The problem was that now I had no place to keep him. For the time being, I decided to give Drew emergency accommodation in a field behind my house while I decided what could be done with him.

One day I went outside to find the three children of the Flynn family in the house next door leaning over the fence, watching Drew. The oldest, Todd, stood protectively in front of his younger sister and brother, and I overheard him saying, "Be careful of this horse. He had to be taken out of Pippy Park because he bit people!"

"But he's such a beautiful horse!" the little girl said, peering longingly over the fence at him.

"He is indeed," I said, coming up behind them. I called to Drew and he trotted over to me. As long as I was nearby the children had no need to fear him and first Todd, then the two littler ones bravely put our their hands to stroke his muzzle.

"What are you going to do with him now?" Todd asked. He looked with admiration at Drew, who once again wore his summer coat of beautiful cloudy grey accented by his flowing dark mane and tail. "He won't have to be—put down, will he?" Todd's voice quavered a little. "They do that sometimes with dogs that won't stop biting people."

"It would be a terrible waste to do that to a fine pony like Drew," I agreed.

"Why's he called Drew?" the little girl, Cindy, interrupted.

"Well, his name used to be Prince, but some people called him Prince Andrew, and it got shortened to Drew."

Cindy's small face wrinkled up in a frown. "He needs a better name than that," she said. "I'm going to think of a new name for him."

Todd persisted in asking, "What will you do with him?"

"What I've decided to do is to have him neutered," I explained. "That's something else we sometimes do to dogs or cats—and to horses, too. When a stallion is neutered, he's called a gelding, and a gelding usually has a calmer disposition—less likely to fight, easier to get along with."

Todd looked back at Drew, now grazing contentedly in the field. "Will it hurt him?"

"Well, he'll sleep during the operation. It might hurt him a bit afterwards for a short time, but he'll soon recover and he'll never know the difference. He'll be the same horse, just quieter and tamer. Of course, we won't be able to use him as a breeding stallion anymore, but he will be able to have a good, long life as a working horse."

"And he won't bite people anymore, right?" asked the youngest boy, Eddie, who had been looking very nervously at Drew.

"That's right—no more biting people!"

In the days after Drew recovered from his surgery, he was happy to graze in the field behind my house. Each day I would see Todd, Cindy and Eddie out there visiting him, bringing him apples and petting him. Eventually all three learned to ride him, even nervous Eddie.

One day as I came out, Todd was just lifting Cindy up onto the pony's back for a ride. "Steady there, Cloudy," she said.

"Cloudy?" I asked. Lately I'd been busy, and the children were spending more time with my pony than I was. Had they already thought of a new name for him.

Todd rolled his eyes. "We *decided* to call him Chief Grey Cloud," he said. Todd had agreed with me that the pony's mane and tail looked like an Indian chief's headdress when he ran. "I thought it was a great name, but little Eddie can't say it properly, so we started calling him Cloudy."

I looked at the pony, now walking gently around with Eddie on his back. He still looked as noble as ever—like a prince or a chief, indeed. But with his lovely grey colour and his gentle disposition, Cloudy seemed like not a bad name for him.

"I think Cloudy is just fine," I told Todd, "though we can always remember that his proper name is Chief Grey Cloud. I think you've found the right name for this pony at long last."

"He sure is good with the kids," Todd said as we watched Cloudy with Eddie and Cindy. He spoke like a confident eleven-year-old, man to man. "But you know, I've noticed something weird? When Mom comes out, he freaks. He runs away and won't come near her."

"It's not just your mom," I assured him. "I've noticed it too. He's like that with all women. Maybe it has something to do with the woman he bit in Pippy Park. He seems to resent women wearing skirts."

"You can't really put him back in a park or anything then, can you?" Todd said. "Because, like, a lot of the people who came to see him would be women."

"I think the best place for him is somewhere out in the country," I said, "away from crowds, where he could work in the fields and the woods and not be around big crowds of people."

I had a place in mind for him. Two brothers, fishermen named Rex and Howard Roberts, were long-time friends of mine down in Whiteway, Trinity Bay. I had talked to them about Cloudy and they were sure they could use a New-foundland Pony. When they met him, they were even more sure. I could tell that they, like everyone else who met Cloudy, had fallen in love with him at first sight.

So Cloudy went to live around the bay with the Roberts family. Rex and Howard built Cloudy a fine new barn, fed him up to perfect condition,and trained him for work in the fields and the woods. Cloudy, the Newfoundland Pony, became their very own "Heritage Animal."

One summer afternoon, twelve years later, I was busy running some messages downtown and was surprised to run into Todd Flynn, now a young man who had grown up and gone away from home, back for a visit. "Dr. Fraser," he said, "I've often meant to ask you what became of the pony we had at your place that summer—Cloudy?"

I smiled at the thought that even as an adult Todd would have fond memories of the pony he had shared for one

Howard and Rex Roberts give Cloudy some work by hauling out the wood for the following winter. Cloudy just loves the opportunity to be out on winter days.

summer. "He's still down in Whiteway with the Roberts'," I told Todd. "I've often been to visit him and he has a great life there. He works hard, he's well cared for and well loved—just like part of the family. Rex and Howard Roberts are two men who really care about their Newfoundland heritage and culture—and their Newfoundland Pony is a living part of that."

I remembered my most recent visit to Cloudy, saying goodbye to him in his paddock and thinking back to when I had first seen him as a tiny colt. His life had been an eventful one, and as I stroked his nose I said, "Well, Prince, or Drew, or Chief Grey Cloud, or Cloudy—it really didn't matter at all what your name was. What matters is that you've finally found the good home you deserve."

Cloudy retired in Whiteway, Trinity Bay

2 Two Survivors

Beauty was an overworked and underfed little pony when my friend Cliff George drew my attention to her. "Andrew," he told me, "there's a pony that grazes by the roadside near my house. I don't think she's been well treated—she's only a tiny thing, and not very old, but she looks completely worn out." One day I went with him to see Beauty, and found that Cliff's report had been accurate. Indeed, the five-year-old pony looked thin and exhausted, but her big black eyes were still beautiful.

I remembered Cliff's father, Esau, an old horseman, saying, "If you want to judge a horse and you can only look at one point of the animal, choose the eyes. The eyes tell a lot. A suffering animal won't look at you properly. Why should it, if people have made it miserable? A creature in despair closes out the world by glazing its eyes and focusing on nothing." But Beauty still had some of her spirit left. Her eyes still glistened and moved. She was still trying to be herself, to hold on to life. She may have been doing back-breaking work, but her spirit was not broken. Her hope was not lost.

"I need to find out who owns this pony, Cliff," I told my friend. "I want to buy her."

It might have seemed like a hasty decision, but I couldn't allow such a fine pony to suffer if it was in my power to give her a new life. Cliff seemed to understand that. "I don't

15

imagine her owners will be too sorry to part with her," he said, holding out a hand as though to stroke the shy creature. "They're certainly not treating her very well."

"There's another reason," I went on. "No matter what kind of horse it was, I wouldn't want to see her suffering, but this one is not only a Newfoundland Pony but a very rare variety, smaller than most. She's special, and she needs special care."

And so Beauty became mine. I arranged to have her brought to a field on the edge of St. John's which would be a good place for her to graze. The field belonged to the university. I also needed to find someone to help care for her.

Margaret, a good friend of my wife's and a woman who was used to caring for horses, was the perfect choice. She took one look at Beauty and knew what the pony needed. "Most of all," Margaret said, "she'll need TLC—Tender Loving Care." Margaret readily agreed to take over the work involved in caring for Beauty, and she and I became partners in the task of bringing this little animal back to health and strength.

I wondered if Beauty had ever before felt a comb through her hair or a brush over her body. After a few weeks of Margaret's care she was looking better with neatly trimmed hooves, a bouncing mane and a smoother coat. She had a fuller belly but the bones all along her back could still be felt sticking up.

It was a very long time before Beauty earned her name again and acquired her proper, beautiful appearance. The colour of her plump body was now a rich dark brown. Her mane, tail and all four limbs were jet black again. Her muzzle was a light fawn colour. She also had smudges of fawn low down on each of her flanks.

Margaret and I stood leaning against the fence in Beauty's paddock one day, gazing in admiration at the fine-looking specimen before us. "Now that you can see her proper colouring, she looks like an Exmoor pony, doesn't she?" Margaret said.

"She has that colouring, all right," I agreed. "But Beauty's ancestors were here in Newfoundland long before the Exmoor pony was recognized as a breed in England. She's descended from the horses of Ancient Britain—a remnant of the early primitive small horses of Europe."

"Amazing," Margaret said. "So, how did her ancestors come to Newfoundland?"

"No-one knows for sure," I said, "but they may have come out with John Guy from south-west England. He brought ponies with him when he came on his second visit in the seventeenth century. She might also have some Sable Island blood in her."

"She really is special, isn't she?"

"Very special—with an impressive history behind her, and hopefully a bright future ahead! What we'll want to do, of course, is find a mate for her."

"Yes, it's about time to be thinking of that," Margaret agreed. "Since she's such a special breed of Newfoundland Pony, it would be wonderful if she had a foal."

The problem was that we had to find a small stallion who matched Beauty's size, and there just weren't any in the area. While Margaret and I made enquiries to find out about possible stallions, Beauty, unaware that we were matchmaking for her, spent her summer convalescing in the secure grass paddocks adjacent to her home stable. On the grass she got even fatter, as ponies do. "It's a carry-over from the Ice-age," I commented to Margaret when she pointed out how plump Beauty was getting. "Remember, I told you she was prehistoric! Ponies fatten themselves on the lush grass of summer in preparation for the lean times of winter to come. Their genes don't seem to know yet that the Ice-age is over."

"It's just as well, living here in Newfoundland!" said Margaret. "We have our own little Ice Age every winter, so I'd say the ponies are smart!"

Summer and fall had passed, the mating season was over, and still, as Margaret said, "We haven't found a husband for Beauty." But just before Christmas, I heard something that looked like it might be the answer to our problem. Word reached me of another pony desperately in need of special care—a young male. Someone had found him in a starved condition and was trying, unsuccessfully, to get him into a better state. I quickly arranged to take the horse into our custody.

If bringing Beauty back to a healthy condition had been a challenge, the young stallion provided a far greater challenge. When we first brought him into the stable, he gulped down a bucketful of water in an instant. "He's even more thirsty than he is hungry," Margaret said, watching as his sides, ribs showing painfully through them, heaved.

"We'll have to ration his water for a few days," I said, "or he may hurt himself, but his drinking habits will soon get back to normal."

His eating habits took a little longer. The poor pony, starved and mistreated, did not know how to eat the good horse food, rich in grain, that we gave him. Once he learned it was good to eat, nothing could stop him.

"Poor thing, he's like an addict," said Margaret one day when I came up to watch the stallion's feeding. "Look at him—he goes crazy when I feed him. Step back—I've found it's better to give him some space when he's eating. It calms him down a little."

"Isn't it incredible?" I said, shaking my head sadly. "To think that someone could treat a pony so badly that he wouldn't even be able to eat good food without almost losing his mind!"

"He's not always like this, though," Margaret said. "Sometimes he's just the opposite—I can comb him, brush him, anything, and he doesn't respond at all. Just like he was a stuffed horse."

But, as with Beauty, time and care began to restore this new pony. Slowly his dead coat of faded, fuzzy hair was shed. By the time Margaret and I were plucking the last tufts of old hair from his body, he was reacting to this with slight annoyance. His new coat was black and shiny. His dignity was being restored along with his health.

"I'm glad to see him getting a little more life in him," I said as I watched Margaret brush him one evening.

She laughed. "More life? That's one way of putting it! It's true, he's much livelier and that's good. But I don't think he appreciates all I've done for him." As if to illustrate her words, the pony lashed out at her with one sharp hoof and Margaret nimbly dodged his kick.

"Should I try him for awhile?" I suggested, taking the brush from Margaret. But I fared no better. The little stallion nipped at me with his sharp teeth.

"You're right, he's not very grateful to us, is he? He'll be happier when he can get outside in spring, I'm sure. It's about time we thought of a name for him."

"Oh, I've already thought of one," said Margaret. "How about calling him Whisky?"

I had to admit, the name suited the pony's high-spirited disposition.

Finally the spring day came when we were able to put this little, shiny, spirited horse out to pasture. "That's what he's been waiting for," I said, watching Whisky canter around the pasture, tossing his shiny mane.

Whisky loved the great outdoors. He was still high-spirited, but he was no longer dangerous as he'd been when he was confined indoors. The winter of loving care had transformed him from a feeble foal to a fiery steed, unlocking his true nature. His genetic characteristics were definitely worth preserving, and a mating with Beauty could put this stallion's good features into another generation of small-sized pony.

Whisky was now mature. He was slightly smaller than Beauty but was still a regular little stallion. He still "freaked-out" when Margaret poured his ration of grain on the grass each day. "I carry a stick when I'm serving him his oats," Margaret told me. "Just in case I need to fend him off." But after his feed he was calmer, and reasonably friendly. Beauty too had a some problems with food. Though she didn't go crazy like Whisky did, she was compulsive about getting her feed. Margaret and I agreed that neither Beauty nor Whisky had ever really gotten over the starvation they had endured in their younger days. Beauty got as plump as a pig but Whisky turned his food into good muscle. They were each about 480 pounds. With his shiny coat and new muscles, Whisky came to look really handsome, and he seemed to know it.

During the second winter Whisky behaved better. No longer did he kick everything in sight or attack any person entering his box to tend him. He became more patient when being groomed. Only occasionally did Whisky give a performance of melodramatic masculinity. He was a mature stud—and most important, he was a father-to-be.

Beauty and Whisky were a good pair and had been in each other's company in the pasture all through the spring, summer and fall. Once or twice we had even seen them breeding. But it wasn't until the ponies were moved indoors for the winter that we got a good chance to inspect them at close quarters. Beauty's belly was clearly getting bigger, and not just from her healthy diet this time. As more time passed, we could sometimes see the foal jumping and kicking inside her. We knew that a birth was on the way.

One Sunday morning, when Margaret went to feed Beauty, there was the newborn foal. It was a filly. She was tiny but as perky as her father. When I came up to see her, I was delighted with her.

"She's the colour of cocoa," I said, and Cocoa became her name. A few weeks later, Margaret told me that the spelling of the foal's name should be changed—from "Cocoa" to "Koko."

"Koko?" I asked.

"Koko the clown," Margaret said. "She's a little clown, anyone can see that."

Even at a few days old she could kick playfully but very competently. When the foal and mother were out in the paddock, Koko would gallop and race flat out, as though pursued by a demon. "All healthy foals love to race around like that," Margaret said with an indulgent smile as we watched her.

When Koko became socialized she was as charming as a fawn, a little delicate creature, innocent of human ways. She had the fibre of her father and the charm of her mother. Koko had been given the best of both parents. This strain of small Newfoundland Pony was continuing with a perfect specimen. It looked like a happy conclusion to the joint stories of Whisky and Beauty, but the situation was about to change.

I was ready to retire, and I knew I would no longer be able to keep Beauty, Whisky, and Koko. I wanted them to have a

Whisky

home where they would be well cared for and their special value would be appreciated. I discussed the problem with Margaret and with other friends who were also pony lovers. We all agreed that a good solution might be to donate them to the university. After all, I worked for the university, and the university owned the field in which they ponies lived. Surely an institute of learning would understand the importance of having what might be the last living specimens of the very smallest Newfoundland Ponies.

It seemed like a good solution, and I donated the pony family to the university, sure that they would be well cared for. Some time went by, and I had not seen the ponies for quite awhile, so I made some enquiries to find out where they were now living.

What I found out made me furious. The three ponies had been sent away—not together, but to three different destinations. The family had been disbanded!

"But where have they gone?" Margaret asked when I told her about it. "And why would they do such a thing—why couldn't they keep them together?"

"I don't know, and no-one seems to be able to tell me," I replied in frustration. "I've asked and asked, but nobody seems to be able to tell me anything about what's happened

Beauty and Koko

to them. Wouldn't you think a university would have more sense? I made it clear to them that these were a special variety of Newfoundland Ponies. If Whisky and Beauty had been kept together, they could have had more foals like Koko! Instead, nobody seems to know where any of them have gone!"

"It does seem foolish," Margaret agreed.

A long time has gone by since then, but I have never been able to find out any more about what happened to the family of little ponies. It was sad to break up a family, and thoughtless to throw away the chance of breeding anymore of these special ponies. When Margaret visited my wife and me recently, she asked if I'd ever learned anything more about Whisky, Beauty, and Koko.

"Not a thing," I told her, and filled in the story of my efforts to track them down. "I don't even know if any of them are still alive," I concluded bitterly.

Margaret smiled. "Oh, I think they're still alive—separately, maybe, but still alive. Think of how much Beauty and Whisky both went through before you got them—they're survivors, both of them. And Koko was just like her parents, full of life and energy. Let's hope all three of them found their way to places where they were well cared for."

I managed a smile in return. "You may be right," I said. "They were survivors. And thanks to the time they spent together here, their variety of Newfoundland Pony will survive too." If Whisky, Beauty, and Koko were the survivors we believed them to be, then the smallest variety of Newfoundland Pony will continue to be part of future generations of ponies.

ठ A Queen in Retirement

Many years ago, in a small harbour near Witless Bay on Newfoundland's east coast, a young couple married and built a house. Mr. Walsh was a fisherman and his wife looked after her house and garden, like so many other young women in the community. Soon they had a baby, Ruby, and just as Ruby was learning to walk, their son Danny was born. One day Mr. Walsh came home from a trip to another community across the harbour, bringing with him a Newfoundland Pony mare.

"She'll be a fine help around the place," Mrs. Walsh said approvingly. "We can use her in the garden for sure."

"And she'll be great for hauling wood in winter," Mr. Walsh said. "What should we call her?"

The little pony looked at them with clear, calm eyes that seemed to promise a good partnership. The name they chose, Queen, seemed well suited to her dignified manner.

Queen quickly found her place in the Walsh's home and in the community. She was a strong horse who could pull heavily laden carts around the harbour and the hillside. From more distant woodlands she hauled countless logs on her bobsled, winter after winter, over snow and ice, to provide fuel for the family wood stove. In the garden Queen pulled a plow, a mowing machine, a long hay cart, or a box cart, according to the season's work. Queen even helped to build

25

the community wharf. She earned her keep and was well cared for.

The years went by and the two children, Danny and Ruby, grew up with Queen as a part of their family. They helped care for her and both loved her. But eventually the time came when they were grown and ready to move away from home. Queen was an older pony by then, no longer able to do the hard work she had once done, but Mr. and Mrs. Walsh decided to keep her as a pet.

In the surrounding community it seemed that no one could remember a time when Queen was not around. She was part of the landscape, except in winter when she lived in a stall in the small barn beside the house. She was truly a full member of the family and a senior citizen in the locality.

Ruby, who had gone away to St. John's to train as a nurse, found a job and settled down there. She only came home on the occasional weekend or holiday. When she did, she always found time to greet Queen and pay her respects to the old mare. Danny had become a carpenter and had worked locally for a while, but after a few years, he too left to take a job in Halifax.

Mr. and Mrs. Walsh were growing older now, and with the work of raising their family done, they were content to stay home a lot. After Danny went away, the fields behind the house became overgrown. Queen wandered around in these fields from May to November. Mr. Walsh, watching her out the kitchen window one day, remarked to his wife, "That pony's lonely, I think."

"I suppose she is," said Mrs. Walsh. "We're not very lively company anymore, and I guess she misses having Danny and Ruby around the place as much as we do. At least we've got each other," she chuckled to her husband. "Queen hasn't even got the other ponies for company anymore." The other ponies that once made up a community herd each summer had all gone off in trucks to uncertain destinations on the mainland.

The days when people like the Walshes needed ponies like Queen as work horses were over. Snowmobiles and all-terrain vehicles had arrived to do the work that horses had once done. Once, work horses had been used all over the world—heavy draft horses like the Clydesdale and the Belgian in Europe and North America, and here in Newfoundland, the powerful Newfoundland Pony. Long after people in other places had stopped using draft horses for work on farms and in the woods, people in Newfoundland were still using their ponies. But those days were over now, and the few Newfoundland Ponies still around, like Queen, were just family pets.

This was when I met Queen. As a vet, caring for work horses had been my first interest. As time passed, my hobby had become the care of pet horses in general and ponies in particular. My elder daughter, Rhona, had a great interest in ponies, and she got me interested in them too. When I arrived in Newfoundland there were still many thousands of ponies living on the island and I became attracted to them immediately. Within one month of my arrival, I had bought one, the colt named Prince whose name was later changed to Cloudy. I spent my spare time grooming and training him. It was then I discovered the inner qualities of this horse. It had good sense, hardiness and friendliness. My fondness for Newfoundland Ponies led me to get two more, Beauty and Whisky. I often thought how wonderful it would be to have my own herd of them.

At about the time I was looking for Newfoundland Ponies, Mr. and Mrs. Walsh decided they were getting too old to look after Queen. I heard about her and heard that they were looking for someone to take care of her. When I went down to look at her, her gentle, dignified bearing impressed me right away. She was a good looker with well developed neck and shoulders and a rich dark brown coat. It wasn't long before I decided she would complete my herd.

"It'll be sad to see her leave here," said Mr. Walsh on the day I arrived to take Queen away. Other people from the village, mostly older folks like the Walshes, stood around watching and nodding in agreement. "She's a part of this town, so she is," a middle-aged man said. "She's been here as long as I can remember."

But how long *had* she been around? She was already a mature horse when the Walshes bought her so many years ago. Queen's age was a matter of immediate concern to Dick, a good friend of mine who agreed to look after Queen. Dick and I had daily discussions about the old mare.

"She moves stiffly in the mornings," I pointed out.

"She walks fine once she gets out from her box to the pasture," Dick said, "but she can't run around with the others."

"The others" were the other three ponies that made up my herd. Queen could force herself to run short distances occasionally, during some of the horse play of the herd, but this was evidently sore on her joints.

"What about Mary?" I asked Dick. Mary was another, much younger mare in the herd, and for awhile she and Queen had been the best of friends.

"Fast company," Dick said, shaking his head. "Queen couldn't keep up with her. She's on her own most of the time now."

"Must be hard on her," I mused. "You can tell she's a sociable pony, and I'm sure she'd love to be able to run and play with the others." I felt sure Queen was sad about the reality of age, but as time went by she developed her own means of coping.

In order to help her mobility we kept her hooves well trimmed. She was regularly cleaned and sometimes shampooed like a lady in a beauty shop. She was dewormed often and she got an occasional course of antibiotic injections when she got an infection. An old teacher of mine in college days used to say, "A horse's mouth is like a window into its age and health," so I frequently examined Queen's mouth and teeth. This was to ensure that she could chew her food properly and also to guess at her age. By examining a horse's teeth, you can usually make a good estimate of its age. If necessary the appearance of the teeth can be checked out against diagrams in horse text books.

But Queen's teeth had us baffled. It was clear that she was over thirty years old, but her teeth type could not be found in my text books. The diagrams in these books obviously did not go as far as Queen's age. They stopped at thirty. Our final guess, after puzzling it out for months, was that Queen was over forty. "I've never heard of a horse over forty," Dick said in amazement. "Have you?"

"I've read of a few that have lived that long, but I've never known one myself. Usually the life span of a horse is twenty years."

Knowing that Queen was so old only made us want to take better care of her. And, as it turned out, she was pretty good at taking care of herself as well. "Queen does everything sensibly," Dick pointed out in one of our discussions. "She lies flat out at night on the bedding in her box stall after she eats her grain, and she lies on in morning until it's time to eat again. And she always takes all her food."

"It's true," I agreed. "It's as if she really knows how to take care of herself. I guess she's had to, to have lived so long." During the day, Queen grazed in her favourite places in the pasture and took shelter among the trees if the weather was not too good. She always took a midday nap. When she lay down outdoors she always went to a sloping piece of land and lay with her legs down hill and stretched out. If the sun was shining she would lie with her underside to the sun. When she wanted to get up she only had to roll her body slightly downhill and she could then rise with ease.

With Dick's help, I got to know Queen very well. I came to recognize the expressions on her face so that I knew when she was content or discontent, comfortable or uncomfortable, glad of my company or wishing to be alone. A young stallion joined the herd and although he mixed with other mares, Queen would not tolerate him near her. With dignity she kept out of minor horse squabbles. Her old joints got no worse and she was never lame but after three years in the herd she moved slowly to and from the pasture.

Dick called me urgently one morning. When I arrived at the stable, we found Queen lying flat out and still in her box stall, breathing very slowly. "Look," said Dick. "The bedding around her hasn't been disturbed. There are no scrapes in the sawdust around her hooves. She's not moved all night."

Less than an hour later, Queen died in her sleep peacefully, dignified as ever. "She was true to her name," I told Dick as we looked down at her body. "She died like she lived—a Queen to the end." I looked down at her and thought of the long life she'd lived—could it really have been forty years? How the world had changed since she was young! This proud old pony was truly a part of Newfoundland history—a queen among Newfoundland Ponies.

4   A Birth

After I acquired my first Newfoundland Pony I soon got to know many more. There were stallions, mares, and geldings of widely different ages. What beauties they were! What I wanted to see more than anything was something that was very rare then—a Newfoundland foal, one as young as possible. Although I had attended many births in other breeds of horses, a newborn Newfoundland foal would surely be a sight to behold.

In time I learned that Ginger, one of the ponies who lived in Pippy Park, was pregnant and soon due to give birth. I spent as much time there as I could, watching Ginger constantly as her time to deliver drew near. Horses usually like to give birth to their young alone and in private, so it's a very special event to be able to witness the birth of a foal. But I was lucky enough to be there when Ginger gave birth to her foal. It was a memorable thing. More than once before I have told the tale about the first birth I witnessed of a Newfoundland Pony, but I am happy to describe it again. The magical picture will stay with me all my life.

One of the staff at the Park had called to tell me that the mare was close to having her foal, and I hurried up to the barn to see her. When I got there, Ginger was very restless. Sweat was breaking out in patches on the sides of her body and on the sides of her neck. She tramped around her wide box, bedded deeply in clean shavings. As the minutes passed her activity increased. She occasionally dug at the bedding with a forefoot. Soon she had the fixed-back ears and the glazed eyes of any anxious horse. She lay down for short spells quite frequently now.

"This is it," I said aloud, though I was alone in the barn. Ginger was stretched out flat on her side so she could strain with all her power. She was sweating so much that the sweat rose off her hot body as steam. Suddenly a rush of straw-coloured fluid ran out of the birth canal. After one very strong strain a foal's foot came into view, in a thin balloon-like bag of fluid.

I felt like cheering at this sight, and watched intently to see the rest of the foal appear. Ginger rested for a couple of minutes and began straining again. The first foot was well out and the second forefoot had now come into view. The two forelegs were being extended close to each other. The foal's nose then appeared, also inside the bag. The mare heaved heavily again and the bag ripped open. The foal was now forced out as far as its brow, and its knees were tucked somewhere under its chin. Another strain pushed the top of the head completely out of the birth canal. The elbows soon followed and the foal slipped further out, slowly but easily. With a gush of more fluid the hindquarters emerged. The foal then slipped completely out of the mare.

The newborn horse lay resting behind the stretched-out mare. It was flat on its side at first. "It won't be down for long," I thought, and sure enough, the foal soon lifted its head and raised its neck off the floor of the stall. It rolled onto its elbows with its forelegs tucked under its chest; soon it struggled to bring its hindlegs under its body.

The foal breathed regularly now, snorting fluid out of its nose and shaking its head vigorously. Its wet, limp, leathery ears flapped against its neck and head until the ears stood up. The umbilical cord, at a spot near the belly, had tightened and, with the next struggle of the restless foal, it parted there without bleeding. The very wet young animal was now free of any connection to its mother. The foal's birth was over.

Ginger soon rose to her feet, quickly turned to the foal and nosed him attentively. Over his head, neck and back went the mare — quickly nosing, licking and touching with her upper lip. "You know that's your baby, don't you?" I said to Ginger as she uttered some low, deep gurgling calls. The foal answered with a throaty infant murmur, and an attempt to stand up.

He was trying hard to stay upright, and keep his balance, but he fell with a thump. The mare stayed alongside, watching and waiting. The next attempt to stand was a success for a moment but the foal was still unsteady. It reached a half-up position for some seconds before falling down again. But he had experienced a new world above the bedding and immediately scrambled to rise again into it. Watching newborn foals do this never ceased to amaze me. Human children take a year or more to learn to walk, but this foal would be up and walking in a matter of minutes.

Sure enough, at the next attempt the foal successfully managed an upright stance and held it stiffly for a moment. Then it made an awkward attempt at walking towards the wall of the box. As he neared the wall he stopped and stretched his neck and head to the limit, to nose it. As though to help his progress and assert himself, he uttered a few more little sounds. He peered around in a short-sighted manner. The mother's underline attracted the drying-out, intense youngster who proceeded to investigate this gateway to the world he wanted to enter.

At first he nosed around the breast of the mare and

The newborn foal

around her forequarters, stretching out his head underneath her. The search under his mother led the foal further between her thighs, turning his head on one side to go deeper into the dark space there. He had lined himself along-side Ginger, with his hindquarters close by her elbow. She turned her head round and touched his rump lightly with her nose several times while he explored for the source of milk.

He had been making sucking actions and sounds for some time now. When he encountered Ginger's protruding teat, engorged with thick, rich milk, he readily took it into his mouth and began to suck more vigorously. The mare adapted her stance to the nursling by relaxing her hind leg on the opposite side to the foal; this turned her milk gland to-wards his searching lips. He fixed his pouting mouth on the nearer of the two nipples and sucked steadily on the mother with neither animal shifting a foot for a minute. He then disengaged from the mare, moving jerkily and blinking his eyes. The little colt then turned and stretched his whole body vigorously.

"There now, that drink did you a world of good, didn't it," I said aloud to the little fellow. Indeed, as he began to explore his box-stall, he managed to walk more steadily and confidently. At times he shook his tail, which he dried out to look furry, more like the tail of a fox. Before long he was back, probing at the mare. She turned her body conveniently for him as she nursed him again. He was now almost two hours old. It had been a long night for both mare and foal.

Suddenly the little fellow was tired. The foal lay down carefully and rolled onto his side, flat out. Quickly he went into a very deep sleep.

The night was February 14th—Valentine's Day. The little foal's caretakers decided to name him Cupid in honour of the occasion. Cupid and I were destined to cross paths again a few years later, but of course I didn't know that on the night of his birth. I only knew that I had been privileged to witness something of the miracle of creation that night.

Cupid's first walk

Cupid enjoying shade and the care of her babysitter

5 A Star in the Woods

Newfoundland Ponies are known for a number of qualities: they are strong, compact animals with well developed neck and shoulder regions, short, strong legs and hard hooves. But more than just their physical characteristics, Newfoundland Ponies are known for their fine temperament, which is one of the best in the whole world of horses. Newfoundland Ponies soon learn what people want from them, and take pleasure in doing their best. By nature, the Newfoundland Pony is an agreeable animal with a positive attitude and an appetite for work. But there's an exception to every rule, including the rule that Newfoundland Ponies are good at their work. One remarkable exception that I got to know was a pony named Star.

I bought Star in the fall of 1982, not knowing what was in store. Star was a neutered male horse, a gelding. He was grey in colour all over. Only his eyes and hooves were black. Little did I know that his mood was generally black also. He was five years old when I got him in Green's Harbour, Trinity Bay, but he did not come from Green's Harbour originally. He was believed to have had his roots in Bay Roberts, the home of many different horse breeds, from other countries. Star's appearance was good, he had a strong look about him with a very solid body and four sound legs.

Esau George and his son Wayne are good friends of mine

in nearby Whiteway. All three of us intended to use Star in the woods at weekends for our supply of winter fuel. Hauling logs out of the woods in winter is the kind of work Newfoundland Ponies usually do well. For many years, when young men and old went into the woods in family groups or friendly partnerships to cut and trim trees for building and for fuel, the Newfoundland Pony was a valued part of the team. Twisted paths through dense, crowded woods gave these ponies no problem. The nimble animals went uphill, round rocks, through narrow trails among the trees, through snowdrifts or across frozen ponds, drawing bobsleds laden with spruce logs over twelve feet long. Sometimes there would be ten trips like this in a day. And the Newfoundland Pony was well suited to woods work—it was, indeed, a star in the role.

Because of this grand history, Esau and Wayne and I had great hopes for Star when he took up his place in the small barn that Wayne had built for him. Esau and Wayne got him ready for work by giving him some extra daily feed, grooming him, fitting him out with harness and getting shoes on his feet. He got titbits of bread and vegetable peelings each evening from Wayne's wife Mary. Our new horse went along with all of this good care and he seemed entirely suitable for the work that was planned. In a practice session one weekend we hitched him up to a bobsled in the yard and all seemed in order. All we had to do was wait for the winter snow to bring home the trees that Wayne had already cut down in the woods on the adjacent hillside.

When the day finally came, Wayne took Star up in the woods to get the first load of wood. He made sure it was a light load, since this would be Star's first time hauling wood, but in spite of that things didn't go smoothly.

"How was it?" I asked Wayne when I arrived later that day.

Wayne shook his head. "Not very good at all. He was hesitating a bit, not all the way but just from time to time, you know?"

"Maybe it's just because he's new at it," I suggested.

"That's probably all it is," Wayne said. "After all, it was only a light load and they told us he was already broken-in."

"And he's strong enough for it, no doubt about that," Esau put in. "Likely he just needs more practice."

So more practice we gave him. We took Star up in the woods again and coaxed him along with a couple more light loads. Again, he seemed hesitant.

"Well, we'll rest him until next weekend," Wayne decided after the third load had been brought in. "Maybe he'll do better then."

He didn't. The next weekend was worse. Once the sled was loaded, Star refused to move at all unless he was led by hand. Wayne took his reins and led him along, and after a few minutes Star picked up his speed and began to run with the load.

"He's going, anyway," Esau said doubtfully.

But not for long. As soon as Wayne stopped running alongside Star, the pony stopped running too. And no amount of coaxing would get him to budge another inch.

"What we have here," said Wayne at last, as we stood around Star in a disgruntled circle, "is a balky horse."

"That's what it looks like," agreed Esau. "I've worked with balky horses before." Esau had spent many years working in the lumber industry in Corner Brook and Grand Falls, and he was used to working with horses of the heavy breeds.

"What are we supposed to do with him?" Wayne asked his father.

Esau shook his head. "All I can tell you, my son, is what *not* to do. It's no good beating him or being rough with him—won't do a bit of good and it might do some harm. But as to what'll cure him—well, Andrew, you're the vet here—is there any cure for a balky horse?"

"None I've ever heard of," I said, reaching forward to stroke the pony's mane. He was such a fine-looking, sturdy little creature, obviously well able to do the work, but the sullen look in his dark eye suggested we were in for a rough day—maybe a rough winter. "There's no known veterinary treatment for a balky horse. We'll have to use psychology instead."

Psychology involved finding some titbits—apples and carrots—to coax Star along. He sniffed at the treats but only looked away.

"We could try blinkers," Esau suggested. "Put blinkers on his bridle—so he'll only look at the path, not at everything around him."

Star resisting work

For awhile it seemed that the blinkers might work. Star got one load back to the house successfully. But on the next load, he was as stubborn as ever. The blinkers didn't make any difference.

We tried everything. We tried lighter and lighter loads. We took turns leading him, thinking that with a different person leading he might be better behaved. But instead of getting better, the pony got worse.

"It's more work getting this horse down the path than it was cutting the fifty trees in the first place," Wayne complained as we loaded another pile of logs onto the sled. As each additional log landed on the pile, Star looked back and grunted. "It's as though he counts them," said Wayne.

Late in the morning, as we were coaxing Star step by step back with another load of logs, he stopped stubbornly. We could not urge him to go on. "Ah, just leave him," Esau said. "Maybe he'll follow us if he sees we're going on without him." It was lunch time and none of us wanted to be late for Mary's cooking. But lunchtime passed and so did the rest of the afternoon, with no sign of Star. At suppertime he came galloping into the yard with the empty bobsled bouncing behind. He had stubbornly stood his ground for hours.

"Well, he's had his punishment—going without his supper," Wayne said as we returned Star to the barn. We were all a little discouraged with the outcome of our day's work.

"And it doesn't seem to have improved his attitude one bit," I pointed out. If missing a meal didn't teach Star a lesson, perhaps nothing would. There seemed to be no more we could do to change his balkiness and his bad attitude.

We gave up our winter work plans and decided to get a different pony for the following winter. Star was obviously never going to turn into the useful working pony we had dreamed of. Wayne later found out that Star had Shetland pony blood in him, which might be why he was not a success as a work horse. Esau eventually found a new home for Star over on Conception Bay.

"Have you heard anything about how Star's doing?" I asked Esau a few months later, over a cup of tea in Wayne and Mary's kitchen.

Esau grinned and shook his head. "Man who bought him, he's got experience with horses, and he thinks Star could be good for a riding pony."

"Riding?" I said. "It's hard to picture Star letting someone sit on his back."

Esau nodded. "That's what I thought. I was up-front with the fella, told him the horse was a balker, but he was pretty sure of himself. Maybe he was right—I don't know."

"All I know," chimed in Wayne, "is that if I go to a horse race and see a horse there named Star—I won't be putting any money on him!!"

Star, the balker, and Wayne his exasperated owner

6 Esau's Last Horse

When I made a home for myself in Trinity Bay, I quickly found a friend in a local man called Esau George. Though Esau was several years older than me, we had a lot in common. We shared a lot of the same opinions, we both loved the old ways and, most of all, we both loved horses. I was living alone at the time and Esau "adopted" me as one of his family. "Drop in any time, b'y," he would say, laying a hand on my shoulder as I left his home, and he really meant it. More and more often I found myself dropping into his house and sitting around his kitchen table. I liked and respected Esau, and I learned a lot from him. He was a living encyclopedia on the old ways of life in Newfoundland, and he also knew a lot about horses.

Esau had spent many years working in the lumber woods where he used big draft horses. Like many outport Newfoundlanders of his time, he had worked hard throughout his life in the woods. During the years he spent logging, he lived in huts and barracks for many months at a time. Many of the men who worked in the woods became expert horsemen leading big horses in the heavy draft work of dragging logs from the woods to the paper mill. Esau was one of these experts.

I enjoyed Esau's tales about these times but I was even more fascinated with his stories about the old days in Newfoundland. He remembered his boyhood very keenly, and tales his father had told him going back to the eighteen-hundreds, were also well preserved in his memory. Esau had absorbed all the pictures of that earlier age, especially if horses were part of the scene. I too remembered stories from the Victorian age, told to me by my grandparents in Scotland, and I had always been interested in hearing more about those days. Getting to know Esau, with his stories about old times and horses, fulfilled that wish.

Horses played an important role in the stories Esau told me—horses and ponies both, for in those days they were all called horses, big and small. It was the age of the workhorse, when virtually all outdoor work depended on pure horse power. As every season brought a different kind of work for the people in the Newfoundland outports, each season likewise meant a different kind of work for horses.

"Springtime was plowing and harrowing," Esau told me, "but that wasn't the only work the horses had to do. They had to cart crops like potatoes, turnips and hay—that went on all year round. Then in June, after caplin spawning, there'd be thousands of tons of caplin piled up on the beach. Folks would load them into boxcarts and take them up to the gardens."

"For fertilizer?"

Esau nodded. "That's right, so the horses would have to haul all that caplin from the beaches up to the gardens, as well as plowing and breaking up the soil. And all the equipment was horse-drawn, of course."

"What about in summer?" I asked.

"In summer, they'd cut hay for the winter. They used mowing machines that were pulled by ponies. There was plowing to do in the vegetable gardens, and they hauled kelp up from the beach for fertilizer."

When the ponies were let out in the Spring to roam all Summer, they would trot and gallop up and down the community to celebrate their freedom.

In late summer, Esau told me, horses were used to haul gravel for the local roads. Outport families also used pony and cart to transport their winter's food supplies home from the general stores of the community merchants.

"Wintertime," Esau said, "now the horses were a real hot topic, you might say, in the winter. Winter evenings, people would meet around in each other's houses, and it usually wasn't long before the talk would turn to horses. Most everyone knew a lot about horses, back then—harnessing, shoeing, breaking, training, breeding and feeding—the whole lot of it. They used to trade stories and information about horses on those long winter nights."

"Winters weren't as busy as spring and summer in the outports, were they?" I asked.

"Busy? Well, all times were busy, back in those days, but with the fishery over for the year, people had a little more free time to visit and to socialize. They used their ponies for the long trips to get food, supplies, and medical help when they needed it. They could travel across the bays by sled, when the water froze, and that would shorten the trip." Ponies were important, too in the social side of outport life, especially in winter. Many rural communities were culturally isolated until they eventually became connected by better roads. Even after roads were built, horses were still needed for awhile because many of the narrow rough roads were only adequate for travel by foot or pony. In winter conditions a pony and sled made it much easier to travel from one community to another. The sled could glide along swiftly and smoothly.

It was in winter, Esau told me, that most of the social events would take place. They could be church or community suppers, plays or concerts. "They were called *times*," he explained, "and people from three or four different communities would all come together for a time. Of course, that was when the horses came in handy again."

But the winter months weren't entirely free of work. It was during the winter that men cut the wood their families would need throughout the year. "That was hard work for the men and for the ponies," Esau said. The men had to keep up the toil of driving the horses and keeping the heavily laden bobsleds on the narrow woodpaths. The ponies stuck to the task. The tracks on the frosted crust could form a trail for them to follow in and out of the woods all day long. Fortunately, the pony was well suited for this work. "They used to fasten sleigh bells to the pony's harnesses," Esau told me, "all different sizes and different tunes. Then, when the logs were loaded on the sled, the pony and sled would go skimming over the ponds. It was a lovely sight and sound—made all that hard work seem easier."

On calm winter days, the arrival of visitors to an outport community was often indicated by the sounds of the sets of bells on the horses. Each small Newfoundland community was such a world to itself that even the sound of sleigh bells from a different place could be detected. On clear, still, cold days, by listening carefully, the people in a small outport community often knew who was coming into the community by the characteristic chiming of the sleigh bells. As Esau described to me the sound of the sleigh bells on the crisp winter afternoons, he shook his head. "Some people say we folks in Newfoundland were behind the times, because we went on using horses for so long after it was all cars and trucks and machinery everywhere else. But I think we were lucky."

"I think you were lucky, too, to hang to that way of life. It seems like the age of workhorses lasted about fifty years longer in Newfoundland than it did in the rest of North America. In spite of all the modern conveniences, you could almost wish those days were back."

"I allow there's a lot of folks feel the same way," Esau said. "I know there's plenty of people still have their ponies just as pets—too fond of them to give them up."

Esau had long since given up active horse work, but it wasn't hard to tell that his heart was still in it. He liked to visit my ponies and to hear me talk about them, and I guessed he wouldn't mind having one of his own if the chance ever came.

It was about this time I once again met up with the young gelding whose birth I had watched in Pippy Park a few years before. He had been named Cupid, and though the name had suited a cute foal, it seemed a bit silly for the strong work-horse he had become. He was a nice, placid pony with a friendly temperament. Geldings generally made the best work horses, so I wondered who would like this young pony as something of a working animal. I wanted to find a good home for this pony. Esau quickly came to mind. Now that he was retired he had time on his hands for such a demanding project.

"Esau, how would you like a pony?" I asked him one evening. "The new gelding I've got—he'd be a good work horse and I wondered if you were interested."

Esau's eyes lit up. "Tell you the truth," he said, "I'd love to have a pony again. It sounds great—but I'd better check with the family, see what they say. It's a big job for an old fella like me to take on, and I might need a hand now and then looking after him. So I'd better make sure they're behind me on this." The experience that Esau, his son Wayne, and I had had with our balky horse Star was well behind us now, and Cupid, with his attractive strawberry roan coat, was a horse of a different colour in more ways than one! Esau's family had no objection to making the pony a part of their lives.

Naturally, soon after I delivered the gelding to Esau's place, I came over to see how my old friend and his new pony were getting along.

"Great pony!" Esau said enthusiastically. "Queer old name they got on him though—Cupid?! I've been calling him Prince."

I laughed, thinking of the young colt I had bought several years ago named Prince, and how I had observed then that Newfoundlanders seemed to call every male horse Prince. Esau was staying true to tradition on that score. That other Prince had ended up with the name Cloudy: now, it seemed, Cupid was going to become a Prince.

"I'll tell you, it's a big change for me," Esau said, rubbing Prince's nose affectionately as we stood in the stall Esau had fixed up for him in a little barn out in the yard. "I worked with Newfoundland Ponies a little when I was hardly more than a boy, but most of the work I did in the woods was with the big Clydesdales, so this is all new to me."

"It would be a change!" I laughed. "Clydesdales can weigh close to a ton, and this letter fellow is barely five hundred pounds."

"But he's a fast learner," Esau said. "Breaking him in to pull a sled or a cart is no trouble at all so far. He's not like that one Star, not at all!" We shared a chuckle at the memory of the stubborn pony. Prince, with his strong, stocky body and a gleam of intelligence in his bright eyes, was eager to work. And Esau was a good owner for him, keeping him well tended and well exercised.

On my next visit, Esau showed me an antique set of sleigh runners he had repaired and told me about his plans to add new shafts, an oak whipple tree and a good set of coupling chains. He gathered up lots of good old parts of harness and made a well-fitting harnessing outfit for the little pony. "It'll be just like old times," he told me excitedly. "We'll have a proper sleigh we can ride in behind this fine little pony."

But although Esau was so fond of antiques, the collar and bridle he bought for Prince were brand new, strongly made with brass fittings. "You didn't salvage these from the olden days," I said, admiring the bridle.

"No," Esau admitted, "some things I'm happy to buy new. You know how important it is for a horse to have a good, reliable harness. But I'm going to deck it out with antiques—a whole set of them!" He held up a string of jingling sleigh bells, all different shapes and sizes.

"Bells! Now that *will* be just like old times!" I said. "Where did you manage to find all those?"

"Oh, I asked around here and there, old fellas like myself who used to work with horses. Everybody had a few lying around—when I put them all together on his harness, I'd say we'll have a fine set."

The day came when the sleigh was finished and Prince's bridle was all outfitted with the jingling sleigh bells. "And if anyone deserves to have the first ride in it, you do," Esau said to me. Prince was harnessed to the sleigh and the loudly jingling rig speedily took off in its first trial run across the big frozen pond nearby, leaving a wake of light snow behind.

The sleigh glided easily and could be turned promptly in any direction. The pony trotted out briskly, responding lightly to the long leather reins in the expert hands it had learned to obey.

That was the first of many magical winter excursions I went on with Esau and Prince. Prince was certainly a good working pony, hauling many sled-loads of firewood for Esau and his family. But I sometimes thought that the pony, like Esau, enjoyed most the days when we were free to travel in the sleigh across the pond and along snow-covered wood-paths. Prince played his part magnificently, as though rewarding Esau for his life-long association with horses. And Esau, the driver and tour guide, loved showing me the beauty of the woods in winter as they could never be seen on any snowmobile or all-terrain vehicle. In some ways, it was like a trip not only across the ponds and through the woods, but back in time.

One evening as we headed back across the pond, I closed my eyes in the gathering twilight, breathed the fresh cold air and listened to those jingling sleigh bells. It was easy, for a moment, to imagine that we were back in the outport days of Esau's youth, or in the faraway times even before that. Esau must have been thinking the same thing, for he said, "There's not many people around today who can have this kind of ride we're having here. This is a piece of history, this is." Gently steering Prince up towards the road, he said, "I'll always be glad you found this pony for me. I've worked among horses all my life, and I never expected to have another one—nor to have one that's given me as many hours of pleasure as Prince has. No doubt he's the last horse I'll ever own—but I'll have to say, he's also the best."

7 Lost in the Woods

Newfoundland Ponies usually live among people and have traditionally helped, with their hard work, to establish human communities. But when ponies, by choice or by accident, have ended up living away from people, in the wild, they seem to usually do very well there also. Over the years I have heard several stories of Newfoundland Ponies that have lived wild in the woods and survived quite successfully.

Though the shoreline of Newfoundland is dotted with settlements, much of the interior of the island is classed as Wilderness Area, and many charterd areas of woodlands are wild and unknown territory to most Newfoundlanders. Here, off the beaten track, animals can live undetected on the rough barrens and in deep forest. Even the wildlife officers of the province can't observe all the creatures that come under their responsibility. In the island's uninhabited places, countless animals survive very well—including the occasional horse.

When Newfoundland Ponies were numerous and lived freely in herds all around the outports it wasn't unusual for a pony owner to discover that his animal was missing at the fall round-up when all the horses were being taken to their home barns for the winter. Sometimes a wider search would locate the missing pony in an adjacent community. Sometimes a missing pony could not be found anywhere and was simply written-off as unfortunately lost. Not all of these were permanently gone. An occasional, strange pony sometimes showed up in another community as the people of that town were rounding up their ponies at the end of October or early November. There was no doubt that lost ponies found new homes in most cases.

One early winter day in the late 1970s, a Newfoundland Pony wandered to an strange destination—St. John's. This pony found himself on someone's property in the city, and of course the person who found him advertised all over, letting people know that a Newfoundland Pony had been found. But no-one came forward with any information. No-one seemed to know who owned the pony, and so the person who found him adopted him. Appropriately enough, she chose to name the pony "Mystery."

Mystery seemed to like his new home, for he never wandered away again. Seventeen years later Mystery is still living in St. John's and has become a bit of a celebrity. He often gets to take part in major parades through the city.

But Mystery's experience is rather unique. Lost ponies are not likely to head for the city suburbs, but for the woodlands. A friend named Mike who lives near Gooseberry Cove on the Cape Shore, and who is very interested in Newfoundland Ponies, told me the story of one pony who lived wild for about twenty years.

"Now this was a long time back," Mike told me one peaceful Sunday afternoon as we exchanged pony tales, "about thirty years ago. I saw the pony myself, several times. The place it lived was inland from St. Bride's in Placentia Bay—a ways down the shore from here."

"What did it look like?"

"Dark grey colour, average size. Nice-looking pony."

"Was it a male or a female?" I asked.

"No-one ever knew for sure," Mike said. "I suppose no-one got close enough to it to be sure, but I think it was a male that hadn't been castrated—a stallion. From what I heard, this pony must've been about three years old when he decided the bachelor life was for him. He was born in one of the communities around there and he had an owner at one time, or that's what I've been told. But no-one seems to know just why he went into the wild."

"Maybe he was difficult to handle—couldn't be trained," I suggested. Having tried to train a balky horse myself, I could imagine how frustrating that would be in a time when people relied more heavily on horse-power.

"Could be," Mike agreed. "Perhaps when the horse went his own way in the fall, the owner just decided to let him have his freedom and didn't bother trying to get him back. Likely as not they just thought it was better to leave the horse to nature and see if he could survive."

"And I guess he survived all right!"

"He certainly did. Sometimes you could see him far off on the barrens in summer, and once in a while he even turned up on the edge of a herd of ponies."

"Did he mix with the other ponies?"

"No, just seemed to watch them from a distance. When the summer was over he'd never try to come near a community, but just disappeared into the woods, and he'd stay there all winter. No doubt he had a sheltered place in there."

"I guess he'd find most of what he wanted in there—he could dig through the snow for herbage, reach up trees for twigs, and find running water."

As Mike and I discussed the pony's life in the woods, we agreed that it wouldn't be much different from the way a moose lives. In wintertime groups of moose have a system of "yarding-up." A group of them dig out a yard for themselves in which to live. These yards are usually among trees and they provide good shelter. Moose do not have to forage far from their yards since they can dig through the snow together to expose vegetation to eat. They also feed off the branches of trees around the winter yard.

A smart horse can dig away at snow and break up ice with its hooves. In fact, the horse's single hoof might serve as a better digging tool than the cloven hoof of the moose. Again, horses have strong upper and lower incisor teeth for biting and pulling at herbage. The moose has no top incisor teeth, although it can manage well enough to bite. We can see, therefore, that a horse is not without the means of surviving winter in the wild, as do moose and other deer of the north. In addition, the pony of this island has stronger, deeper rooted, molar teeth than most other breeds of horses. This feature allows the pony to grind up tough food for good digestion.

"So this pony just stayed out in the woods all through the winter, and never came near people?" I asked.

"Well, almost never," Mike said with a grin. "He had his limits, it seems, for sometimes when a winter storm got too severe he'd show up outside people's houses in St. Bride's, looking for a handout!"

I laughed. "I bet he got it, too."

"Oh, he sure did. People would give him food—his favourite thing was bread and molasses. When he had enough he'd go back to the woods and they wouldn't lay eyes on him again until the next bad storm. It was the only time he ever came into a community. Some winters, we wouldn't see him at all."

Mike told me that as the years went by, the pony continued to live in the wild. Sometimes the small number of people who knew about the horse presumed that it was dead since it had not been seen for a long time. Then it would be reported seen once more.

"By the early '60s, there were no more reports of anyone seeing the pony," Mike said, "but it was years before people finally believed it was lost in the woods for good. No-one ever found his body, so we never knew where or how he died."

"It makes you wonder, doesn't it, how many other Newfoundland Ponies lived in the woods like that, over the years."

"It does indeed. And it shows what a hardy breed they really are," Mike agreed.

On the Burin Peninsula, in more recent times, a group of snowmobilers one winter saw a Newfoundland Pony deep in the woods a long way from Marystown. All other horses in

Living in the wilderness

the area had been taken indoors for the winter. This animal was clearly lost; no one had reported a missing horse to the Mounties. It was a strange situation and nobody knew what exactly should be done.

Many people said that once the winter got worse, the horse would make its own way home. They didn't realize that most Newfoundland Ponies are quite comfortable even in the worst of Newfoundland's climate. Some ponies enjoy being loners when they live outdoors. This Marystown pony appeared to choose its winter freedom and disappeared further into the woods.

About two months passed and everyone forgot about the wild-living pony. But later in the winter, another group out on their snowmobiles came back with another report of the wild-living pony. "We saw him!" they told people. "He's in a very remote place though, a place where you couldn't go on foot."

"We think he may be trapped in there," another added. "If the place can't be reached on foot, how could anyone get in to take him out?"

"You can't take a horse out on a snowmobile," someone else pointed out. There didn't seem to be any way to rescue the pony, if indeed he was trapped.

The story was discussed around the community until it came to the ears of a man named Arch Kelly. Mr. Kelly heard about the pony in the woods and said, "I don't mind trying to get in there on foot and take a look at the pony. I can see how he's doing and if he needs help."

It was a brave offer to make, but it was typical of Arch Kelly. He was not only someone who loved and knew ponies, but also a kind, generous man who was willing to go out of his way to help others—a real Good Samaritan.

Mr. Kelly got himself ready for the long journey—a

twelve-mile trek through the snow. The snowmobilers hadn't been able to pinpoir.t the exact spot where they'd seen the pony, and of course, he might not still be in that place, but Arch had a pretty good hunch where the animal might have decided to stay, and he set out for that spot.

After a long, hard hike through the winter woods, Mr. Kelly reached the area where he thought the pony might be. Sure enough, there were signs of grazing and hoofprints in the snow. Before long, Mr. Kelly caught a glimpse of movement through the trees. He walked quietly in that direction and, sure enough, there was the pony.

The handsome bay coloured pony lifted his head at Mr. Kelly's approach. "Hello there, fellow," Mr. Kelly said softly, hoping not to startle the animal. He certainly looked to be in good condition—far from starving, he was even plump. Obviously even in the middle of winter he'd found plenty to eat.

Mr. Kelly had thought the pony might be a bit wild and hard to approach, but instead, it seemed quite tame. Rather than shying away, it trotted towards him.

Mr. Kelly stroked the pony's mane as he looked it over more carefully. "You're doing fine, just fine, aren't you?" he said. "How would you like to come home with me?"

The pony didn't resist as Mr. Kelly brought out a halter and leading rope to put on him. Together pony and rescuer set off back through the woods, toward a road that would take them back to Marystown.

The pony travelled well and stayed close to Mr. Kelly. For quite a while they made good progress, but then Mr. Kelly stopped. Ahead he could see a deep, wide cleft in the snowy ground which marked the course of a river.

"Well, this is quite the fix we're in," he said aloud to his new friend. "It'll be dark soon, and there's no time to turn around and look for a detour. We'll have to get across this somehow." He led the pony closer to the edge of the cleft and looked down at the rushing water below. Mr. Kelly was a strong, athletic man, but even he could not clamber down the steep, frozen side. And even if he could have, what would the pony do? They would need a bridge.

Fortunately, Mr. Kelly had prepared well for this trip into the woods, and among his equipment was an axe and some cord. He quickly felled three trees nearby. He chipped off the branches and bound the three tree trunks tightly together. Then he dropped them across the cleft and pushed them down until they were wedged securely.

"It's not much of a bridge, but it'll have to do," he said. He patted the pony reassuringly before setting foot on the make-shift ramp. "I'll go across by myself first to make sure it's safe."

The log bridge held steady as Mr. Kelly went across alone and came back for the pony. He took the leading rope and began to coax his new friend out onto the bridge. The pony seemed very nervous, but he trustingly followed Mr. Kelly, keeping his nose pressed against his rescuer's back all the way across.

It was slow progress, for Mr. Kelly didn't dare hurry. Inch by inch he and the pony stepped across the creaking wood that separated them from the dark, cold water of the river. They had to trust each other. If either one slipped, both could plunge into the river and be killed.

It seemed to take hours, though it was only a few min-utes, before Arch Kelly's boots touched the firm surface of the bank on the other side. Carefully he led the pony up off the bridge. They had made it!

Off they hurried homewards. There was still a long walk ahead in the gathering dark, but they encountered no more obstacles and finally they were out of the woods and back in familiar territory, heading for Arch Kelly's barn. Both tired and equally ready for supper and a roof over their heads, the man and the pony entered the barn. "This is it," Mr. Kelly told the pony. "This is your new home, if you're satisfied to stay here."

And the pony was happy to stay there, along with Mr. Kelly's other horses. He had survived well in the wild, but perhaps he had learned to appreciate the comforts of home while he was out there, because he settled in quickly and made no attempt to run away. One thing was certain—that pony was devoted to Mr. Kelly. It would do whatever he asked. Today, the pony from the woods still lives with his rescuer, and the bond of friendship between the two is something everyone remarks on.

Recently, in a very different part of Newfoundland, a beautiful, blue roan coloured, yearling colt named Clyde was due to be put out on summer grazing. The colt had lost its mother and needed new companionship. Clyde was the son of the famous stallion Skipper and had been born and raised near Whitbourne, but there seemed to be no suitable company in the neighbourhood for a young male horse. It seemed like a good idea to team up Clyde with another young male horse and to let both of them spend the summer together in a secure location. After some searching, a match was found for Clyde. Another young male pony from the isthmus, the area where the Avalon Peninsula meets the rest of Newfoundland, was also ready to go out grazing for the summer. Clyde could have a buddy.

The plan was to put the two young ponies out on Crawley's Island, offshore of Long Harbour, Placentia Bay. Ponies had been summered there on the two previous years with reasonable success. The only real advantage to putting ponies on an island is that you don't have to put up any fences. However, you also can't visit them as often to inspect them and see how they're getting on. You just have to put them on the island and wave goodbye until your next trip across the tickle. In spite of this, Clyde and his buddy were bound for Crawley's Island. A mistake, however, was in the works.

The best plan probably would have been to introduce Clyde and his buddy, get them used to each other as a pair, and then take them together to the island. Instead, Clyde was brought across the tickle alone. It wasn't an easy crossing and Clyde found it stressful. When he got to the other side, his caretakers left him there on his own and went away to get the other horse.

When they arrived back on the island with the second pony, there was no sign of Clyde anywhere. He was already lost in the woodlands of the uninhabited island.

"Well," said one of the men, when they had all agreed there was no hope of finding Clyde, "we'd better just leave the other one here. They'll find each other soon enough."

The "buddy system" is quite a common way for horses to relate together. If two horses are paired and there are no others to interfere, they will form a partnership. Together they go through their daily routines, enjoying the safe presence of a companion. Almost every horse likes to have a buddy, though some horses choose to be loners. Some horses live quite successfully as loners, but for the most part, horses are very social creatures.

Days went by, and some helpful local people scanned the shore of Crawley's Island with binoculars to see what was happening over there. The second colt could easily be seen, but there was no sign of Clyde, so clearly the two had not buddied up together. Someone volunteered to take a boat

Vision of an old pony living in the woods

around Crawley's Island to see if he was on the far side. There was no sign of Clyde, but one of the volunteers went up onto the island to have another look for him. Again, no luck. It was clear that Clyde was lost.

"What could have happened to him?" I wondered as I discussed the mystery with the others who were caring for Clyde. "He's young and inexperienced—he might have met with an accident. He could be lying in the woods with a broken leg."

"Or he might have tried to swim back home," someone else suggested. We were all haunted by fears of what might have become of him.

Something had to be done to track down the missing pony. The suggestions included plane searches, helicopter touch-downs and radio appeals. Eventually a sensible suggestion was made to put a good search party onto Crawley's

Island with a plan to fan out and search it thoroughly. There were numerous volunteers for this and a trip was organized.

Clyde was found deep in the woods towards the back of the island. He was very easily caught. He had made a little home-base for himself in the woods near some marshland. The location provided him with food, water and shelter and he seemed quite settled there. His instincts had taken over and taught him to survive. He seemed contented, yet he was happy enough to be led away. Down on the island's shore-line, where grazing was plentiful, Clyde was now properly introduced to his intended buddy. The two formed a bond fairly quickly and they had a good summer together.

I am now convinced that there exists, in this breed of pony at least, an instinct for independent survival in the wild. When this takes over, for some reason or another, the pony in question may appear lost to us but it only has gone back to nature. We should perhaps remind ourselves that this species did very well in nature for millions of years before we domesticated it. Horses undoubtedly need our care today but some, it seems, are still quite prepared to try to manage

Clyde the loner

8 Skipper and Friends

In 1992 I had a few Newfoundland Pony mares and decided it was time to think about getting some foals from them. That meant finding a stallion to breed with these mares. As I told my friend Cliff George, "I've just published a book about the Newfoundland Pony, telling people that the pony is on the point of becoming extinct. Now I feel like it's up to me to do something practical about it."

Cliff, an artist who had painted many pictures of Newfoundland Ponies he had known, joined me in many daily excursions in search of a stallion. On the Southern Shore we could not find a single stud. Around Placentia Bay we found no stallion. None existed either in the area of Trinity Bay. We then concentrated on Conception Bay and soon heard of one near Bay Roberts. We tracked it down only to learn that it had gone on "the meat truck" two weeks before.

"What a waste!" Cliff said to me as we drove back from that unsuccessful trip. "Imagine someone selling a Newfoundland Pony stallion for dogmeat. Do people realize how rare the breed is?"

"It seems as if some people don't," I agreed, "though perhaps that stallion was old or in poor health. Surely somewhere we'll find a young, healthy stallion to breed with the mares."

Even after such a long, fruitless search I was optimistic

that we would eventually hear of the stallion we were looking for. Soon we heard of one near Carbonear. Cliff and I
drove out to see him. "Great horse, great horse," the owner
said enthusiastically as he led us down to see the animal. Sure
enough, he was a fine, healthy Newfoundland Pony, but the
owner was disappointed if he hoped to make a sale.

"There's just one problem," I said. "We were looking for
a stallion, and this horse is definitely a gelding!"

The owner looked shocked for a moment, but when I
explained that I was in need of a stallion I could breed with
my mares, he laughed and admitted that, unfortunately, he
had had the pony castrated recently. It was a good little
gelding, but no use for what I needed.

Cliff and I laughed too, as we drove away from that little
excursion, though we were still frustrated. "We finally find a
stallion, and it turns out not to *be* a stallion any more," I said.
"What worse luck can we have?"

"A friend of mine told me the other day that someone had
a Newfoundland Pony stallion for sale in Conception Bay
South," Cliff said. "I'll make some enquiries and we'll check
that one out. Maybe that will be our lucky day."

After asking around a little, Cliff got the name and phone
number of the man with the pony for sale. I gave him a call.

"I hear you have a pony stallion for sale?" I asked.

"That's right!" said the muffled voice on the other end of
the line. "Do you want to see him?"

"Yes, I'm interested. You see, I have a herd of Newfoundland Pony mares that I want to breed. This pony is definitely
a stallion?"

"Absolutely," the man assured me.

"And you're sure it's a Newfoundlander?" I asked, for a
pony of another breed would not be much use in trying to
carry on the Newfoundland Pony breed.

"Of course he's a Newfoundlander! He's from Bay Roberts! When can you come out and have a look at him?"

The next evening found Cliff and I squeezed into a pickup truck with the stallion's owner, off to see the pony. The road was very rough and it went on for miles. The evening was getting dark when we arrived at the remote barn.

"This is where you keep him?" I asked.

"That's right. People bring their mares out here to breed with him," the stallion's owner said, pulling the truck to a stop. It seemed like a secretive, almost eerie place for the stallion to be kept, but perhaps for the business he was in, he preferred a little privacy, I thought with a smile.

"Now you wait by the truck," the owner said as we got out, "and I'll go in the barn and bring out the horse."

He was gone a few minutes, then he and his stallion together came out of the barn.

"Oh, no," Cliff said under his breath. "Looks like we've struck out again."

Even in the dim light we could see that, while this horse might be a true Newfoundlander from Bay Roberts, it was certainly no Newfoundland Pony. It was a huge Clydesdale nearly twice the size of a pony. We explained the problem to our new friend as politely as we could, and got out of there.

"Now, there's a man who obviously does not know the meaning of the word 'pony,'" I said to Cliff as we sat in the cab of the pickup, waiting for the owner to put his horse away and drive us back home.

"Probably, like a lot of people, he just thinks it's another name for a horse," Cliff pointed out.

But a pony is a special kind of horse and a Newfoundland Pony is a special kind of pony, in the opinion of those of us who are very fond of this natural breed. A pony is a small-sized horse. It may be young or old, but it must be less than 145 centimetres in height when it is fully grown, which is normally at five years of age. Most Newfoundland Ponies are around 125 centimetres high. In addition, ponies have usually thick-set bodies and short shins. They do not have long hair around their feet, nor do they have big hooves or long ears as the Clydesdale had. One great feature on a Newfoundland Pony is undoubtedly its heavy winter coat. This starts growing in the fall and is shed in late spring. The coat sometimes changes in colour by the seasons. Nearly every Newfoundland Pony also has a nice personality.

I had a chance to point out some of those differences to the stallion's owner on our ride back, and he left us knowing a lot more about Newfoundland Ponies than he had when he picked us up. But we were still no better off in our search for a pony stallion.

But I didn't give up looking. In the old days when herds of Newfoundland Ponies roamed freely about the communities, mares and stallions bred together and new foals were born each spring. No-one had to worry, back then, about finding a stallion to breed with their mare. But those days were long gone. If the Newfoundland Pony could have any future, it would be the result of breeding by special arrangement. Without further breeding of this kind, this previously natural breed would soon be dead.

My search for a male pony continued, taking me to Clarenville, Gander and Fogo Island. I drew a blank everywhere and I began to fear that no more pony stallions remained in the island. But my luck took a turn for the better when I told my story to Peter, a reporter for *The Monitor*, a newspaper based in St. John's.

"That sounds like a story people might be interested in," he said. "And if it were in the paper, there's a much better chance that someone who has a Newfoundland Pony stallion might read it and get in touch with you." Peter interviewed me thoroughly, asking all kinds of questions in order to get the full picture for the article he intended to write, When it came out in print it occupied a full page and asked readers, island-wide, to supply information on any pony stallion known to them.

The power of the press made all the difference. Peter's article pointed out that without such a stud to breed with the mares, the Newfoundland Pony would soon become extinct. When people read that, they began to get interested.

Some days after the newspaper article, I received a phone call from a man in Marystown on the Burin Peninsula.

"My name's Art," he told me. "I'm an RCMP sergeant, but I'm also a horseman. Somebody showed me the article in *The Monitor* about how you were looking for a stallion."

"A Newfoundland Pony stallion," I hurried to point out, wanting to avoid any errors like we'd made with the man in Conception Bay South.

"Well, I know where there are two good ones, down around here. I think I can arrange for you to buy them, if you're interested."

"They're for sale?" I asked, getting excited.

"I think they could be, if the price is right," Art said.

"That's wonderful news," I said. "This could be the end of a long search for me."

Art went on to tell me that one of the stallions was a six-year-old grey in need of special care. "The owner lives alone and he's been sick most of last winter, so he hasn't been able to look after the pony like he should. The pony hasn't been properly fed, but us RCMP officers down here have been looking after him and trying to help care for him. But he needs extra care now."

I never could resist a horse in need of care, and when Art assured me that the pony was basically in good health and could become a fertile stallion if he was well cared for, I said, "Why don't you see if you can arrange for me to buy that one, Art?" The other stallion would be available for another buyer, and indeed it was soon bought by someone else interested in breeding ponies. I got the six-year-old; little did I know I was acquiring the most lovable stallion that I had ever encountered.

When he arrived at the place in Conception Bay that had been arranged for him, he looked gaunt. He weighed 560 pounds, according to the measuring tape. His ribs stuck out and his sides were hollowed-in. But the skinny stallion was a proud fellow with an air of dignity. When my wife saw him, she said, "He's got a long ways to go, but he'll make it. He looks like he's got a lot of spirit."

"I think so too," I agreed. "What should we call him?"

"How about Skipper?"

Skipper

The name suited him, and a friendly skipper he was when he got to know you. He had taken his hard times in his stride.

Skipper's new friends, including Cliff and me and several others, rallied to help bring him back to health. The horse got very well fed and some necessary medical attention in an excellent barn in Torbay. Once he had gained weight—he now weighed 640 pounds—and was in good condition, we moved him to Green's Harbour, Trinity Bay, where he joined four mares. He bred with these mares and each one gave birth to a foal the following year. Skipper was now the proud father of four foals so beautiful that they attracted hundreds of visitors and many new Friends of the Newfoundland Pony.

The Friends of the Newfoundland Pony help by donating time, attention, accommodations, or funds in order to provide good care for any pony that needs it. The "Friends" have helped to buy a few ponies being offered for sale who might otherwise have been sold for meat, like the unfortunate pony in Bay Roberts that Cliff and I had just missed seeing. The "Friends" now own three male ponies and breeding has begun with two of these. A few mares have been gathered up as breeding stock, and the "Friends" have found hay, some of it donated by kind horse-lovers in New Brunswick, to feed the ponies while in their various winter quarters.

As more and more people learn about the needs of the Newfoundland Pony, more of them are getting involved. Some people have agreed to take in ponies to live with them—they are acting sort of like "foster parents" to these ponies. Ponies are also being offered for long range adoption to people living some distance away from the action.

Another project for the "Friends of the Newfoundland Pony" is a permanent sanctuary for Newfoundland Ponies. Discarded ponies, old ponies, breeding stock, geldings, all need a location where they can be cared for. Very recently a lovely twelve acre pasture land surrounded by sheltering trees, has been rented by the "Friends" as a good sanctuary in Conception Bay South. A herd of eleven ponies is now living there.

Meanwhile, what about Skipper? Well, he has produced his second crop of foals and has proved himself a perfect stud. He is now being cared for by Mrs. Gloria Thorne, a very experienced horsekeeper at New Harbour, Trinity Bay. It was in Mrs. Thorne's company that I went recently to see Skipper, along with my friend Cliff who had joined me in the long search for the perfect stallion.

"He loves his mares," Mrs. Thorne pointed out as we watched Skipper with his herd, "and he's very protective of them if any intruder comes by."

"Yet he still looks like he's a friendly horse," I said.

"Oh, very sociable, to his friends," Mrs. Thorne said, and to demonstrate she called Skipper over to us and we all patted his mane.

"If anyone needs an advertisement for the Newfoundland Pony," Cliff said, "Skipper is the best there could be."

And, in a way, Skipper has been an advertisement, because he has made several appearances on TV around Newfoundland. He is one of the best known Newfoundland Ponies on the island. "Well worth the long search we had for him," I said to Cliff.

"And let's not forget who finally found him for us," Cliff said. "They say the Mounties always get their man, but in this case, the Mounties got our pony!"

Two of Skipper's Mares

9 The Black Stallion

"That's my father who has the pony," the young man on the other end of the line replied. "He's not here right now, but I can tell you about the pony."

"It is a stallion?" I asked.

"Yep, a black, six-year-old Newfoundland Pony stallion."

"Has he ever bred any mares?"

"None, but he's capable of it. But we've just kept him as a pet here on our dairy farm. Would you like to come out and see him sometime?"

"I think so," I said. Another healthy, six-year-old breeding stallion who was truly a Newfoundland Pony seemed too good to be true, and I had my doubts. Maybe I would be disappointed, as my friend Cliff and I had been on the many trips we'd taken before we found Skipper. In my short talk with Bill Hoskins' son, I hadn't been able to find out how much the young man really knew about horses. After all, it was a dairy farm, so perhaps they were experts in cows instead! I hoped this wouldn't be another fiasco like our visit to the Clydesdale, but I needed to check it out myself to see that this really was a Newfoundland Pony.

Just about that time, the CBC decided to get involved in the story of the Newfoundland Pony. "Land and Sea" de-

cided to do a show about the plight of the pony and the search
for stallions. When Pauline Thornhill, who was organizing
the show, talked to me about it, I happened to mention that I
would be going soon to visit a possible breeding stallion on
Random Island.

"That sounds interesting," Pauline said. "It would fit
right in with the program—trying to find a new stallion to
keep the breed going, getting everyone's reactions when
they see the pony—do you think our camera crew could
possibly come along and film the visit?"

"I don't see why not," I said, "but we'll have to check with
Mr. Hoskins.

Bill Hoskins, when we finally got hold of him, agreed to
have the CBC camera crew come along with me on my visit
to his farm.

The trip was arranged for a day at the start of summer.
The CBC team travelled in their own vehicle and Cliff George
joined me in my car following the television people. "I
thought you should be along," I told Cliff, "after all those
unsuccessful trips we took together looking for stallions.
This trip should be a little more fun."

"And it'll be our moment of fame," Cliff pointed out.
"When we see this on TV, it'll make all those earlier trips
seem worthwhile."

We stopped along the way so the camera crew could get
a few shots of Random Island in the distance across the clear,
sun-splashed waters of the bay. At the same, time, we all got
a snack. As we ate, Cliff and I chatted with the TV crew,
learning a little more about their work and what they were
looking for in this program. It really made us feel like part of
a team.

"There's just one thing I regret," I told Cliff as we got back
in my car to drive on to Random Island.

"What's that?"

"I wish I'd worn a tie."

"Why? It's not going to be very formal—we're going to a dairy farm, after all."

"I know," I said, "but I can just picture myself in front of the camera, straightening my tie, hamming it up a bit, you know?"

Cliff shook his head and chuckled. "I hate to break it to you, Andrew, but I think they're going to be a little more interested in the pony than in you!"

But as we drew nearer to the Hoskins place, I began to see things in a more serious light. When this pony went in front of the camera lens, it would be a real moment of truth. The program wasn't scheduled to air for several months, but today's shooting would be the beginning of something that might make or break the cause of the Newfoundland Pony. Suddenly, it wasn't just good fun. It was all much more serious.

The TV crew raced on ahead to set up the equipment on the dairy farm where the horse had been housed all winter and spring. He would only be let out, for the first time that year, when we were all suitably assembled in the farm yard.

When I arrived the TV crew was still setting up so I took the opportunity to introduce myself and Cliff to Mr. Hoskins and his son. "Do you want to look at the pony before they start shooting?" Mr. Hoskins asked. It seemed like a good idea. True, Pauline had made it clear that she wanted the camera to capture everyone's honest reactions when they saw the horse for the first time, but I still wanted to check him out first, to be sure he was all I'd been told he was.

The little stallion was in a stall in the dairy barn; instead of other horses for company, he had cows all around him. He was jet black with big dark eyes, and he was fat from all the cow feed that he got in addition to his hay. After looking him over, Cliff and I retreated to the farm yard to await the release of the stallion.

Out came the horse like a Mack truck on the highway. The young man on the end of the stallion's head rope was being dragged along as fast as he could run. I could see why the crew had wanted to keep him in the barn until filming began, because his sudden burst into freedom made great television. After a circuit of the farm yard this black body of pent-up energy slowed down a bit and I was able to approach him. In spite of his fearsome entrance the horse seemed approachable. I knew nothing about him yet, but I felt I could trust him. We met each other face to face and touched noses.

The camera behind was taking in this encounter, but I had to ignore it and concentrate on the horse. Close up to him like this I could feel his personality. The horse's black eyes were kind. His big soft muzzle went all over my head and shoulders in gentle touches. He extended his face out to mine in an offering of instant friendship and trust. I knew he approved of me and my heart went out to him. We were buddies already.

As I fondled the animal's head and stroked his neck I started to examine him more seriously. I already knew I liked him and he liked me, but I was here on serious business, finding out if he would be a suitable stallion for our needs. He was a Newfoundland Pony alright with the regular height, the typical strong neck and shoulders, short back, broad forehead, deep jaw, small ears, black and shortish legs, low tail, deep chest, and compact hooves. I felt up between his hind legs and verified that indeed he was a stallion and not a gelding. His front teeth showed that he was young and had a good broad bite. His mane and tail were long with ropy tangles. Some tufted remnants of his old winter coat stuck to his lower chest showing that it had been a very heavy coat, of the type that is the hallmark of Newfoundland Ponies. While I examined him and the camera crew pulled in for close-ups, Cliff stood in the background, quickly sketching the pony.

"He's a bit too fat," I said aloud, knowing the TV crew wanted to hear my reactions, "but it's better for a pony to be too fat than too thin after the winter and spring is over. Spring's a hard time for ponies, when the winter hay is scarce and the new grass hasn't grown yet. They need extra horse feed to keep them going till summer comes."

"I guess you could go too far with it, though, couldn't you," an interviewer asked.

"Oh, by all means. Like any other animal, a pony's not healthy if he's too fat. But this one looks to be in good shape."

Our newly encountered black stallion was certainly a happy animal. We let him off the rope and he scampered away to the nearby pasture at a full gallop. After he had gone some distance he returned to us racing flat out. We tried to recapture him and at first he avoided us, but he didn't go far. When he came close enough, I got my arms around his neck and he pulled up very obediently.

"So, what do you think of him?" Bill Hoskins asked, obviously proud of the great TV debut his pony was making.

"I'd like to steal him!" I said wholeheartedly. "He'd make a wonderful pet, but I think he's got a different future ahead. Black stallions are considered among the most handsome of horses and this is the only one of its kind in Newfoundland." I had only just acquired my own grey stallion, Skipper, and I couldn't take on this one as well, but I was confident that his discovery by television would give him a new status and a new career, and I told his proud owner so.

The *"Land and Sea"* program on The Newfoundland Pony was shown in the fall. I watched it from the comfort of

The Black Stallion

my living room and enjoyed every minute of it. Plenty of other people watched and enjoyed it too, as I found out when viewers began to respond.

The program had included Skipper too, with details about the hard shape he had been in when I first bought him, and his happy recovery. Most viewers loved the scenes of Skipper chasing around and bucking, but for older horse keepers "around the bay" the scenes of this Black Stallion on Random Island were the highlight of the show.

That was because of all the ponies included in the program, The Black was thought by many to be the most hand-some and the first choice as a potential breeder. Before long my phone began ringing with people from all over the prov-ince asking me for more details about the black stallion. "I've got a Newfoundland Pony mare," one woman told me, "but she's never had a foal. Do you think I could bring her to Random Island and breed her with the Black Stallion?"

The Black had no proven ability as a stud, but his the TV program showed that he was obviously handsome and fit, and I received many other calls from people like that woman, people in Bay Roberts, Whitbourne and Conception Bay South, who wanted to make bookings for their mares to go to the Black Stallion at his Random Island home. Just as I had predicted to Mr. Hoskins, the Black had a full-time career.

My friend, Bill Kennedy, took two of his mares to The Black. One of these, Belle, he was especially excited about. "She's a black mare that looks for all the world like a copy of the stallion," he told me.

"Really?" I said. "A foal from those two would be a beautiful animal—and a great prospect for the future New-foundland Ponies."

In late summer I paid my third visit to the Black Stallion. After our first meeting in front of the TV cameras I had gone to see him a second time, so we could get better acquainted in private. He had been at pasture on a reduced diet for a while and was down to a normal weight, and he seemed to be very well contented. At that time he was out of the barn and staked-out near his owner's house.

On my third visit, I found the Black Stallion living in relative freedom with two mares as his companions. "Has he bred the mares?" I asked Bill Hoskins.

"I couldn't say for sure, because they're not always right

around here," Bill replied, "but people say they've seen him breeding both mares."

"I suppose only time will tell if the mares are pregnant," I said, watching the Black from a distance. He wasn't as friendly as he'd been before, but that was because all his attention was taken up with his two mares and his need to protect them. "That's normal for a stallion with mares," I told Bill, thinking of Skipper and his little herd out in Green's Harbour. "The Black still looks good though, doesn't he?" His shiny black summer coat glistened over his forequarters and strong, masculine neck.

A brief appearance on TV had brought the Black Stallion not only a new life and a new career, but a lot of new friends and fans. And all of us were waiting eagerly to see what foaling time next year would bring.

10 National Maggie

A few years ago, one Sunday in the fall, my wife Bernice and I set off on one of our periodic trips round the Southern Shore and the Cape Shore of Newfoundland's Avalon Peninsula. This time we had a special reason to take this scenic tour through coastal communities with colourful pasts. We were going to take a look at a young pony that had been advertised for sale in the newspaper of the previous day.

"We're really not going to buy another pony, are we?" my wife said. She appreciated horses as much as I did, but was sometimes dubious about my eagerness to own almost every pony I saw.

"Not this time!" I assured her. "I'm just curious. It's been a long time since I've seen a pony for sale."

"It will be nice to have a look at it," she agreed.

The area we were driving through had once been famous for its excellent ponies, but that was long ago when there were many hundreds to be found there. A few hundred ponies still lived among these southern outports up to a dozen years before the time of our trip. But no longer did they roam around. So the rarity of a pony added extra interest to the day's excursion. Would this young horse be a link with the past? Would this pony be as good as its ancestors?

It was a sunny Sunday morning, and an air of peace seemed to lie over the communities as we drove through them. The sea washed the shores with rinses of white frothy waves. The horizon of the Atlantic was an unbroken line of ocean meeting sky. Over that horizon had come the Irish people who had settled these shores. That was many generations back, but the old cultures still remained with them.

As we drove along the shore towards St. Mary, I began to hum the tune of that haunting, beautiful Newfoundland song, "Let me fish off Cape St. Mary's." My wife joined in, both of us thinking of the heritage of this shore. Ponies were a part of that heritage. Although these were fishing communities, the people knew a lot about horses and livestock—knowledge that was a heritage from their Irish ancestors. Perhaps this was how their adopted horse had won its splendid reputation. Horses can be a reflection of their people.

"Well, this is the area," I told my wife as we pulled into the small community where the pony was for sale. "I don't know exactly where, though."

"You'd better ask directions."

I pulled over to the side where two young men were walking down the road and rolled down my window to ask my way. They quickly directed me to the home of the pony's owners and in minutes we were pulling up to the house.

A middle-aged man came out and, when I told him we'd come to see the pony, smiled. "Maggie's back here," he told me, leading my wife and me to the barn. As we went inside, he nodded at a big, dark mare standing in the corner. "That's Maggie's mother," he told me. "The foal's just been weaned. Here she is."

And there indeed she was, a furry foal tied in a stall in the corner across from her mother. I ran my hands over her as the owner told me about her. As we humans talked, the young pony flicked quick, curious glances at me. She didn't seem timid, exactly, but she was certainly a little shy.

"She looks good—nice build," I told her owner. Maggie still had her thickish foal's coat that was mid-brown in colour. Her legs were darker; her mane and tail were black. She stood very upright and had an alert, smart appearance. When I wanted her to move, she responded quickly and I could sense her intelligence. And all the while her big, dark watchful eyes stayed fixed on me. I couldn't help being caught up in a memory—this first meeting with Maggie reminded me so much of a day ten years ago when I'd first met a foal named Prince, the foal I had bought on first sight and who had gone on to lead such an eventful life. When I met Maggie's dark eyes, I had the same feeling I had had ten years before with Prince—this was a pony that was meant to belong to me. It was almost spooky.

But there was one big difference. I had come out here today planning only to look, not to buy a pony. The knowing smile on my wife's face suggested she already knew how captivated I was by Maggie, but all the same I told the owner, "The thing is, I'm not really in the market for a pony right now."

"No? Just came to have a look, did you?" He didn't seem very worried. "We've got some other people coming out to look at her today; I think they're pretty serious about buying."

That clinched it for me. There was no time to go home and think about it—if I didn't act now, Maggie would never be mine. Once again I found myself buying on the spot a foal who had already decided I would be hers.

"Well, after all, it was a good deal," I told my wife in the car on the drive home.

"A very reasonable price," she agreed. "And they're such

nice people." Maggie's owners had invited us in for lunch and had quickly become friends.

"It was good of them to agree to look after her until I can find a place closer to St. John's for her," I added.

As it turned out, Maggie spent another winter at her old home in St. Mary's, while I looked for a good place to keep her. I decided to consult my friend Bill Kennedy, a prominent horse-keeper in Conception Bay South. Bill was a big burly man and a genuine horse-lover. Like me, he was interested in Newfoundland Ponies; in fact he was one of a group of people called "Friends of the Newfoundland Pony." His barn seemed like a good home for Maggie.

"I'd be glad to take her," Bill said. "She'll get the best of care, I can promise you that."

Bill was as good as his word. When I first brought Maggie to his barn that spring, she looked a little lean and rough-coated beside the four plump, well-groomed ponies that were Bill's pride and joy. Maggie's former owners hadn't mistreated her, but they weren't experts at horse care like Bill was.

"She's got the best stall in the barn," Bill assured me when I came down to visit Maggie. Sure enough, her stall was wide, with a springy wooden floor, and it was tucked into a well-insulated corner with the hayloft overhead.

"How is she settling in?" I asked.

"She's a bit shy compared to the others," Bill said. The other four ponies had been residents of Bill's barn for some time and they were all comfortable and confident with each other. "But she'll soon settle in," he assured me, and so she did.

Maggie soon responded to her five star care. She was well fed and was regularly brushed and combed. Never a day

Young Maggie

went by but the filly was spoken to kindly. She was stroked and patted by hand whenever anyone passed her.

As often as possible I visited the young horse and helped to care for her. Like a real lady, she loved a trip to the "hairdresser" so I spent lots of time combing out her mane and forelock, which had grown long as she matured. While I combed her, Maggie would rest her chin on my shoulder.

"You've come a long way, haven't you girl?" I'd say to her, stroking her silky mane affectionately. No longer was Maggie shy or unsure of herself. She was a confident three-year-old who could take care of herself among the other ponies. And she was ready to go out to pasture in company with other horses.

But finding pasture for a horse like Maggie was not the simple task it would have been fifty years ago. Back then, the

coastal communities along the Avalon Peninsula all had
large pony herds that wandered the shores all summer long.
Ponies were important to people back then, so no-one
minded given the ponies freedom to graze around the dis-
trict. If people wanted their gardens protected, they built
fences around them to keep out the roaming groups of ponies
that dotted the landscape.

All that had changed when noisy snowmobiles and all-
terrain vehicles took over the woods and seized the freedom
that ponies had earned with their hard work. The ponies lost
their summer freedom to roam, and their numbers became
fewer and fewer as there was less pastureland for them.
Instead of putting up fences to keep the ponies out, people
now had to build fences around their pastures if they wanted
to keep ponies in. By now, with so few ponies around, the
fences around those old pasture lands were broken down
from neglect. So, a grazing place for Maggie was not easy to
find.

But in Green's Harbour, Trinity Bay, there was an horse-
loving character named Thomas who still kept a small herd
of three old ponies. They grazed a broad, steep hillside
overlooking the harbour. They lived there all year round,
surrounded by sheltering trees. Thomas fed them daily
throughout the winter, proud to be able to preserve a few
good specimens of the traditional breed of pony. Thomas
was also one of the Friends of The Newfoundland Pony.

Bill Kennedy agreed with me that Maggie, along with a
couple of other ponies, should be added to the Green's
Harbour herd for the following six months. During that
summer Maggie showed that she had grown up in more than
just size and self-confidence. She was a fully mature mare
now, ready to breed with a stallion and have a foal of her
own. When, as fall drew near, the little grey stallion Skipper

joined Thomas' group of ponies, I decided it was time for Maggie to become a mother.

"After all, if we're concerned about the future of the Newfoundland Pony, it would be great to get a foal from a healthy young mare like Maggie," I told Thomas.

"I don't think that'll be any problem," he assured me. "Maggie and the stallion have taken to each other just fine."

On my next visit out to Green's Harbour, Thomas told me that while Maggie had bred with the stallion earlier, when he had approached her again lately she would have nothing to do with him. "She liked him fine before," Thomas said, "so if she won't take him this time, I'd say it could only mean one thing."

"She's already pregnant!" I exclaimed with delight.

"Looks like she could be."

And indeed, our hopes had come true. At the beginning of winter, we moved Maggie, who was definitely pregnant, back to Bill Kennedy's barn. Or rather, back to Bill Kennedy's place, but into a brand new barn.

"Running water, electricity, all the latest gadgets," Bill assured me as I led Maggie into the new barn, "and, especially for the mother-to-be, a maternity ward! Takes up a good quarter of the floor space, but I'm sure she'll be glad of it soon enough."

Maggie had been well cared for before, but now she got extra-special care. Besides being clean and well-fed, she got lots of extra treats such as apples and carrots. Before I went to Bill's place to see Maggie, my wife would often give me a loaf of bread for Maggie. "Remember now, she's a pregnant lady and she needs special treatment," my wife would say as she handed me the bread, which was one of Maggie's favourite treats.

Pregnant Maggie

"Is it raisin bread this time? You know that's what she likes best."

"A full loaf of it," my wife assured me. It was a good thing too, because Maggie could eat a loaf of raisin bread in no time.

"Well, I'll bring this treat down to our 'well-bread' horse now," I joked.

When I got to Bill's barn, Bill himself was there tending to Maggie. "You know, I've gotten awful fond of this horse," he admitted as he helped me feed Maggie her raisin bread.

"I don't think it's possible to avoid it," I said. "Everyone who has anything to do with Maggie gets fond of her. She's such a sweet-natured horse."

"Most of the time," Bill said. "Once in a while, when

something bothers her, I've seen her flick out a hind foot at me or someone else. But she usually misses. I think she just wants to remind us she's a real horse."

"And soon to be the mother of another real horse, we hope," I said.

Bill frowned. "I've been wondering, you know—for the longest time, her belly doesn't seem to have been getting any bigger. Are you sure there's a foal in there? I know it takes eleven months, but still—she's not gotten very big."

"I'd noticed that too," I told him, "and that's why I've come down today. I think it's time for me to do an internal examination. Some mares don't like having it done, but I think Maggie'll be all right."

Sure enough, gentle Maggie didn't seem to mind her examination at all, and I had good news to report to Bill. "I definitely felt the foal in there!" I announced. "I could feel the head and legs. There's no doubt, Maggie's going to be a mother!"

Bill and I, and all Maggie's friends, were so pleased by the news that it was hard to stop talking about it, especially to our "horsey" friends. All the Friends of the Newfoundland Pony were informed that pony breeding was again under-way. In the past six years, very few pony foals had been born. Maggie herself had been one of those few—and now she was getting ready to carry on her breed.

Before long, news of Maggie's pregnancy spread far outside our circle of pony-loving friends. Reporters began to call, looking for information about the Newfoundland Pony who was going to have a foal. Many people knew that the breed was nearly extinct, and everyone was excited to hear about this new hope for the future. Along came TV crews to Bill Kennedy's barn, looking for Maggie.

Maggie's first TV appearance was on the popular provincial show "Land and Sea." After that, word got around, and soon Maggie was featured in the TV news. But even after all that publicity, I was still surprised when I heard about Maggie's "big break." When I called Bill Kennedy and told him we'd have to get Maggie ready for another TV appearance, he was as shocked as I.

"Maggie's going to be on 'Midday'?!" he repeated. "Sure, that's nationwide—isn't that the big CBC news program from Toronto?"

"It certainly is," I said. "You'll have to start now getting Maggie ready! This is a big deal—the show will be beamed directly to Toronto and Maggie will be on TV live all across Canada."

I was certainly excited. The story of the Newfoundland Ponies had been well covered in the provincial media by now, but national TV was something else altogether! Maybe if people all across Canada found out about Maggie, our provincial pony would be on its way to being recognized as a legitimate breed.

When the big day came, Maggie didn't show a trace of nervousness. "She's an old hand at this now," Bill explained to the CBC cameraman.

"In fact, she's better at it than her owner is," I admitted. "All this still makes me a big nervous, but it doesn't bother Maggie one bit."

Sure enough, Maggie stood patiently and kept still as I held in position so the camera could get a good shot of her nice head and good figure. As questions from the CBC TV anchorman in Toronto, Dan Matheson, were fed into my ear by headphone, and I did my best to answer, Maggie looked up into the camera from time to time with her big dark eyes. I slipped her a few titbits of cut-up apples to let her know she was doing a good job.

"That was great," the cameraman told me as he came up afterwards to shake my hand and stroke Maggie's mane. "And this one here is a real little professional."

"That's right," Bill said. He grinned at me. "You know, there were moments there when you looked nervous, but Maggie—she was as cool as a cucumber."

I laughed too. "It's been a pleasure working with you," I said, shaking hands again with the crew.

Later that day, when I was back home, my phone rang. It was the "Midday," studio in Toronto. "What did they have to say?" my wife asked when I'd hung up.

"Oh, just to say how much everyone in the studio loved Maggie, and to wish us luck with the new foal," I said. "Of course, I told them they were great to work with also—I really enjoyed doing it. It was a thrill being interviewed by Dan Matheson—but do you know what would be an even bigger thrill?"

"Bigger than going on national TV with your pony?" my wife chuckled. "I can't imagine. What?"

"Going on national TV in the morning—on 'Canada AM'," I admitted. "I'd just love to be interviewed by Valerie Pringle."

My wife laughed aloud at that. "Yes, she's your favourite TV host, isn't she? I'll admit, she does do a good job. Who knows, maybe she'll be interested in Maggie too."

It seemed like a far-fetched wish, but to my astonishment, not too long afterwards, I got a call from Valerie Pringle at CTV's "Canada AM." She was interested in doing a piece about Maggie! Maggie's national fame had reached its peak.

We decided to bring Maggie down to the beach for her "Canada AM" interview, so that viewers across Canada could see the beautiful coastline that was the home background for the pony and all her ancestors. The program was shot there. Valerie drew out the story of this breed and, in her expert way, drew attention to Maggie's lovely features.

Of course, after all this attention in the media, viewers across Newfoundland and Canada were eager to find out what would happen on the long-awaited day when Maggie's foal was finally born. Bill and I, growing more excited as the big day drew near, felt good to know that people around the country were interested in Maggie just as we were.

When Maggie's foal, a beautiful little female, was born, she and her mother were soon on TV again, along with Bill. CTV news carried the story nationwide to the country. Maggie was now Canada's number one pony. And her daughter looked good on TV too!

Maggie's filly gets more like her mother every day, but I think she'll find as she grows up that Maggie is a tough act to follow. Probably no other Newfoundland Pony will ever be such a national star as St. Mary's Maggie.

The proud parents of TV fame

11 Bell Island Ponies

Bell Island is one of the many attractive islands off the coast of Newfoundland—a convenient one to visit for those of us who live in St. John's, since it is quite near the capital city. The first time I visited Bell Island, many years ago, I came away with two different impressions of the island. For many years the people of Bell Island made their living from an iron ore mine which has since shut down. The dead iron ore mining operation left a sad impression, since the community is no longer thriving as it once was. That's the main impression many people get of Bell Island—that it is almost a ghost town. But with my interest in horses, I saw something else. Bell Island has a number of good horses and ponies, and their presence made me feel good about the place. I went back as often as I could to visit those horses.

On my visits I usually made a circular tour of Bell Island. There was plenty to see and enjoy. I enjoyed the trip over on the ferry with an occasional whale or an iceberg to see between the island and the beautiful shoreline of Conception Bay. After leaving the town of Wabana I drove through woods, fields and farmlands. From spring to fall there were plenty of livestock to be seen grazing most parts of the island. These were chiefly cattle and ponies. Seldom did I notice a pony without stopping to look at it closely and often to take a photo. On most visits I would find at least one pony that I had not seen before.

If I stood admiring one of the island's ponies, someone would usually come up and start telling me about the animal. Many people on Bell Island have a good knowledge about horses. One of these people was Leo Byrne, who keeps several horses there.

On one of my visits to Bell Island, Leo Byrne and I were discussing Newfoundland Ponies. "Folks around here," Leo said, "don't make a big distinction between one breed and another, or between horses and ponies. To us, a horse is a horse."

"I notice most of the horses around here seem to be mixed breeds."

"That's right. We don't worry much about breeds—the important thing is what a horse can do, not how it looks."

Leo's point of view was a traditional one about horses. "After all," I pointed out to him, "it's only a little over a hundred years ago that the whole idea of forming breeds of animals took hold. The idea is now, of course, that all horses of the same breed should look the same." The goal was to have animals with certain abilities easily identifiable on sight, and to achieve this, animals who had the desired qualities were bred with each other. As a result, all the offspring looked alike, and it became very important for them to look as much alike as possible. Breed societies began to regulate and document breeding, and animals were registered with pedigrees. Within the recognized breeds, animals are judged by their appearance alone.

"That's not how it used to be," Leo reminded me. "In the old days, animals used to be judged by what they could do, not how they looked. You judged a cow by how much milk it gave, or a dog by how good it was at rounding up sheep, or a chicken by how many eggs it laid."

"And a horse could be judged on speed, strength, or willingness to do what the owner wanted of it—the horse's reputation was more important than how it looked. But if you bought a horse from someone you didn't know, outside your community, how would you know what kind of reputation it had? Maybe that's one of the reasons breeds became important," I finished.

"That could be," Leo agreed. We were in his pasture as we talked, looking at his horses and ponies. My thoughts wandered, as they usually do, to the Newfoundland Pony and this whole question of breeding. What are the qualities that make a Newfoundland Pony? Most of them are sociable, placid, and tough. Do they all look the same? Well, yes and no. They all look similar in general appearance, but they have differences in build, and there are definitely differences in size. "If we started regulated breeding to create a new breed of Newfoundland Ponies," I wondered out loud, "would we have to eliminate the ones who were too different in size? Or should they be kept as part of the pony's heritage?"

Leo smiled. "I don't think most folks around here would worry too much about that. They like variety in their horses."

"How many horses would you say are on Bell Island, Leo?" The island is quite small; you can drive around it in half an hour.

Leo leaned forward, obviously interested in this subject. "About fifty years ago there was a good two or three thousand horses here," he said. "Now, there's less than forty—of all kinds, that is, horses, ponies and all."

"I'd say quite a few of those are Newfoundland Ponies," I said. "I've seen some very good ones on my travels around Bell Island."

Bell Island's history is tied up with the iron ore mines, which began there in 1895, but horses are a part of this history. Horses were needed to haul the ore tubs back and forward, in and out of the mine, on the tracks that went all through the tunnels.

For this work, the miners used big work horses up to 2000 pounds. They were mostly Clydesdale-type horses from Nova Scotia. They were used in the mines until the 1950s when they were replaced by small engines. By that time, many Bell Islanders had become expert horsemen as a result of working with these animals for many years. Their mining era was also a work horse era. Even today, people in nearby parts of Newfoundland often go to Bell Island when looking for good horses to buy.

I was interested in getting a Bell Island pony for myself, but so far in my visits I had never seen a suitable one that was for sale. One day, my friend Cliff George told me about a big Newfoundland Pony in Torbay. "It's a striking-looking pony, and supposed to be a good worker, but the reason I mentioned it is because it's originally from Bell Island," he said. "I know you've been interested in getting a Bell Island pony."

He was right about that, and naturally I went to find the pony and her owner. I couldn't miss the pony—when I followed Cliff's directions, I found her grazing in a field by the roadside. She was a big mare, about 950 pounds, slightly overweight due to lack of work and too much good food. The pony's colour was a beautiful grey roan. Her head and lower legs were darker and her face had a brownish tinge to it. She had a really powerful appearance with her very well developed neck and shoulders, a broad back and a large, solid set of hindquarters. Her big kindly eyes suggested a good disposition. This was just about the very best pony mare in the province. I decided that it was essential to find her owner, Mr. Whitty.

Joe Whitty lived nearby. Not only did he own this beautiful mare but he loved her. I could tell that as soon as he began to talk about "Dolly."

"I got her on Bell Island a few years back," he said. "When we got the ferry terminal in Portugal Cove, I walked her all the way to Torbay."

"You walked her to Torbay? But that's a day's walk!" I exclaimed.

"That's right," he said gently, "but I didn't like to put her on a truck—didn't think it would be good for her." Joe cared about Dolly beyond words—and beyond her ordinary needs. The pony was given good housing, good food, good bedding, grooming and lots of human company and attention.

In Joe's kind custody the mare had learned to do all kinds of farm work. Dolly was a very confident animal and feared nothing. People in the community would borrow her for a variety of jobs, all of which she did willingly. She worked

Joe Witty and Dolly at work

well in all conditions, in all weather, in each season. Dolly did not function like some muscular robot; she was intelligent and used her own good judgement in dealing with any difficulty. She was a contented animal and clearly appreciated her conditions.

"Some people say I spoil her," Joe confessed in his quiet voice, "but they don't understand horses." He was right. Horses are sensitive. They need good care and kind handling to become good horses with kind dispositions. No one could deny that Joe Whitty's horse was one of the best around.

Very tentatively, I asked Joe if the mare might ever be for sale. I almost hated to ask, since he was obviously so fond of her, but I just had to know.

He gave me a penetrating look. "I'd have to think about that," he said. "What would you want her for?"

I told Joe of the plight of the Newfoundland Pony. "The large size of these ponies, like Dolly, have practically disappeared," I said. "Dolly is the last of her type in this part of the world. There are few enough good Newfoundland Ponies now, and none of her size. If she could have a foal, her type of the breed could continue in a new generation."

"Dolly's no youngster," Joe warned me. "In fact, I've been thinking it's time for her to retire. I didn't give her much work this year, but people around who know her still want to borrow her for jobs from time to time. I'd planned on letting her retire altogether at the end of the fall."

It was still early summer. "I'll tell you what," Joe said after we discussed it further. "Why don't you come out and see her a few times over the summer? If you still want her, you can buy her at the end of the fall."

"I know I'll still want her," I assured him. "I can pay you now if you want." We had already agreed on a very fair price for the mare.

Joe waved my chequebook away. "No, no, wait till the fall," he insisted.

My next move was to find a new home for Dolly and, after that, the right stallion for her. Once more my friend Bill Kennedy came to the rescue. He agreed to keep Dolly in his barn for the following winter. At the end of October I bought Dolly from Joe, and Bill moved the mare into his barn with three other ponies. What a precious barnful this was. There was the big handsome Dolly, the medium sized Belle (a solidly built black of excellent proportions), the sprightly, young, bay coloured Maggie, and the smallish bay mare, Daisy, who was Maggie's half-sister. We had each type of Newfoundland Pony under one roof! These four mares could play a major role in restoring their breed. Stallions, however, were missing from our plans.

In the following year both Skipper and The Black Stallion were discovered and we could visualize three of the mares going to them, but they were all too small for a large mare like Dolly. We kept looking, hoping to find a bigger stud to breed with Dolly. The obvious place to search for one was on Dolly's old home, Bell Island. Back there I went again.

I had heard a rumour that there were two young male ponies over there that were not yet castrated as geldings; one of them belonged to my horse-loving acquaintance Leo Byrne. The first one I found was a six-month old son of a racehorse; he would not do. But Leo's pony was a big yearling and he looked like the answer to a prayer.

But Leo wasn't sure. "I'm planning to have this one made into a gelding," he said. "I'm training him to work in the woods—and I've already made arrangements to have him castrated."

I looked longingly at the strong young pony, knowing he was exactly what I needed. "What's his name?" I asked.

Blaze, the Bell Island stallion

"Blaze," said Leo. "He looks like he's going to shape up to be a good worker. Good working ponies aren't easy to come by. But you know he'll be no good to me if he's a stallion."

I knew Leo was right. If a stallion was working in the woods and met a mare while they were both harnessed up, there would be chaos in the woods and probable injury. Only a gelding would be suitable for Leo's plans.

"If there were more good working ponies around, I wouldn't mind," Leo said. "But like I say, they're scarce."

"Good Newfoundland Ponies of any kind are scarce," I agreed. "That's why it's so important to breed them. It's hard enough finding a good work horse, but it's even harder finding a good stallion—especially one this big. Would you let me examine him before I go?"

After I had given Blaze a thorough examination, I was sure he was the horse we needed to breed with Dolly in another year, when he was fully mature. Leo still wasn't convinced, but he agreed to meet me again to talk about it.

When I went to Bell Island again, I went armed with my recently published book on the Newfoundland Pony. I brought a copy to Leo and talked with him some more about the breed and how it was near extinction. Though Leo had earlier pointed out to me that Bell Island horsemen weren't very interested in the different breeds of horses and ponies, he understood the special situation with the Newfoundland Pony.

"I'll tell you what," he said. "I can see you need Blaze, and I need him too. Let's compromise. I still want him as a gelding for work in the woods, but that can wait. We'll let him mature as a stallion and breed a few mares next season. After that I can see about having him castrated."

"That's wonderful, Leo," I said. "You definitely deserve to be called a Friend of the Newfoundland Pony."

"I'd be proud to be one," he replied.

The following spring, when Blaze was first put out on the pasture, I wondered how he looked now that he was two years old and a mature stallion. At that time I had the company of a veterinarian from Cairo, Dr. Atef Mansour, who was on an extended visit to Newfoundland. Atef was an expert on the Arabian breed of horse. I invited him to come with me and give me his opinion of Blaze. We both enjoyed the ferry ride and found the stallion grazing on the far side of the island. Blaze looked like a different horse in many respects but I still could recognize him. "See the white band of hair above his left hind hoof?" I pointed out to Atef. "That's Blaze, all right. But he's become much heavier and quite a bit larger."

Blaze's neck and shoulders were powerful. His chest was big and his back looked strong. His head also had a heavier look, but the eyes were the same. His face and his small pricked-up ears gave him his usual expression.

"He looks like an ideal stallion to breed with your mares," Atef said. "He's an excellent horse. Get some foals from him, at all costs."

Leo, now that he was committed to the project, threw himself into it enthusiastically. He established a newly fenced breeding area big enough for the stallion and several mares to live together for the summer season. We told a few owners of mares about this breeding facility and four or five of them sent their animals over to Bell Island for this purpose. Along with them went Dolly, returning to her birth place, her native soil. She travelled well and seemed happy with the whole arrangement.

Dolly bred with Blaze and spent most of the summer with him before leaving for the "mainland" of Newfoundland. "She's going to Green's Harbour, Trinity Bay," I told Leo when I went to pick her up. "We've got several other Newfoundland Ponies over there that she can spend the winter with."

"Well, you'll have something to look forward to in the spring," Leo said. Although he had originally wanted Blaze to be a gelding, he seemed proud of his horse's success as a stallion and just as eager for Blaze's upcoming fatherhood as I was.

"The foal should be born in May," I told him. "It'll be a foal of pure Bell Island breeding."

"Another Bell Island pony," Leo said. "Well, that is something to look forward to."

12   The New Generation

In the eyes of TV viewers across Canada, the new generation of Newfoundland Ponies began when Maggie gave birth to her precious foal in 1994. Maggie had been watched by television cameras from CBC and CTV during the last two months of her pregnancy. When her foal arrived the cameras pounced.

Bill Kennedy had been looking after the pregnant Maggie and he became drawn into the birth of the new foal. It was a wonderful discovery for him when he found the freshly born foal standing beside her mother when he entered the barn early one morning. The foal was already dry and standing up firmly. The most exciting part of the discovery was that the foal was a female. Reports from other parts of the island told us that three foals had already been born that year, but they were males and a new generation of females was needed. We had found enough breeding males by now, but most female ponies were quite old. For the breed to continue, new mares would have to be born to replace these old ones.

Bill and Maggie and the new foal appeared on the national television news. Canadians could now feel reassured that the tide of extinction, threatening to drown the Newfoundland Pony, had turned. The foal was clearly of national interest and of provincial importance. Since she was an offshoot to Maggie, the foal was called Meg. Scores of visitors came to the Kennedy barn to see her.

Bill and I studied Meg intently for her first month of life. We examined every aspect of her and we liked what we saw. She had her mother's reddish colouring and her father's face and temperament. She had beautiful big dark eyes that came from some other part of her ancestry. Bill was a very proud godfather.

"So, do you think Maggie's a good mother?" I asked him when I came up to the barn to visit mother and daughter one day.

Bill had been watching Maggie in action with Meg, who was growing up fast. "I think she is," he said, "although she hasn't got any experience at the job. Sometimes she gets a little *too* enthusiastic."

"I guess that means you've been kicked, have you?" I asked with a chuckle. Maggie was indeed very protective of Meg, and I could imagine how she might react to anyone who came between her and her foal.

"Oh, she let fly with her hind hoof once or twice," Bill admitted. "But she probably just wants to remind us to be careful. There haven't been a lot of foals born around here for a long time, so maybe we need to be reminded that horses are pretty good at self defence!"

While we talked, Meg trotted over to investigate me. "She's friendly, isn't she?" I remarked. No doubt Bill's kind custody had taught her to trust people. The experiences a horse has while growing up are very important in making a nice horse.

Meg spent a good winter with her mother in the cosy barn. When she was about seven months old she got her own stall where she slept at night. She still spent the daylight hours with her mother in the adjacent "maternity ward"—the large, corner pen where she was born. Meg weaned herself off her mother by the time she was eight or nine months old. Her weaning was helped by the fact that she had long since learned to eat horse feed and hay. She was kept very well fed.

When Meg was about ten months old I came out to visit the ponies one day and found Meg and Maggie in a paddock near Bill's barn. Grass had not started to grow there yet, but they got hay and plenty of freedom in this open space. At first, as I approached, I wasn't sure which pony was Maggie and which was Meg. Meg had grown so much she was almost the same height as her mother. Meanwhile, Meg had acquired two half-brothers and a half-sister. They had been born "round the bay." Like Maggie, they were Skipper's offspring and all were magnificent foals. Skipper had proved himself a great sire for this new generation. His other daughter was born in Green's Harbour, Trinity Bay and she had been named Newfie. This foal was owned by Thomas March, a long-time friend of ponies. Thomas kept Newfie and her mother in a field beside the road near his store. In a phone call he told me that the road was a dead end, "but it's some busy now!" he assured me.

"Why?" I asked.

"People are driving up here all the time to get a look at Newfie. I'd say there's been a thousand people have come up to see the foal since she was born."

"That's wonderful! It really shows people are taking an interest in the Newfoundland Pony."

All the Friends of the Newfoundland Pony were very encouraged to learn how much interest people were showing. One of those Friends was Gloria Thorne from New Harbour, Trinity Bay. Back in 1980, Gloria had been the first secretary of the Newfoundland Pony Society. Now she was a leading figure in the Friends of the Newfoundland Pony. She kept account of what was happening in this new era of pony care, and she was especially interested, as we all were, in the foals born in this first year of renewed breeding.

Ten proper pony foals were born across the whole island that year. Two of these unfortunately died at an early age from causes unknown. This happened in places where Gloria and I had no involvement, so we didn't know the details of what had happened. This left eight foals, of which most were male. Not every foal was typical of the breed's new specifications in appearance. According to pictures printed in the press, one had a big white face and another had four white legs. These were not typical colour features of the new "emerging" breed, though they had occurred in the past. But Gloria, comparing the stories and pictures of the new foals, was not inclined to be critical. "Every foal is a valuable addition to the population," she would remind us. We did not want a new breed, we just wanted the old breed to remain. And it began to look as though it would. Other mares were now being bred to the stallions we had discovered and more foals would therefore be born in the next year of renewed breeding.

That exciting first year closed with Pauline Thornhill doing another television show in the "Land and Sea" series. This show concentrated on the foals of the ponies that had been on the previous program. Once again, the ponies performed like the stars they were. The message of the program was that the breeding of ponies was neither fast nor easy, but the future of the Newfoundland Pony looked fairly good. Meg was only a few days old at the time the show was made, but she looked good. Since then she has developed into the most attractive, affectionate young pony you could hope to meet.

Three of the principal stallions were now Skipper, Blaze and the Black. While the first year's foals were being admired, these three studs and a couple of others elsewhere, were busy breeding additional mares. This would ensure next year's crop of foals. Once again, hopes were high that many of the mares would conceive.

Bill Kennedy helped me to give five of these mares internal examinations. "Well, that's it then," I said after our examinations were complete. "Three are pregnant, but two aren't. Not too bad, I guess."

"Especially when you consider that the other two are older mares," Bill said. Although the older mares were capable of breeding, their chances of success were reduced with age.

"Breeding is a business for the young, after all," I agreed. There were several other mares around in the pony community that we did not examine. Time would tell if they were "in-foal". We certainly wanted at least one foal from each of our three principal studs. We waited through the winter in hope.

The first foal of 1995 was born on Victoria Day, in May. Naturally, when Gloria saw that the foal was a female, she immediately named her Victoria—or Vicky, as she ended up being called. Vicky is Skipper's daughter, a half-sister of Meg. Vicky's mother, Annie, was rescued from the meat truck at Baie Verte Junction. Gloria pointed out to me when I first saw Vicky, "She's a female version of Skipper."

"You're right," I said. "She's got that same deep grey colour. Meg looks more like her mother, Maggie, but Vicky is just like her father." She has a nice, somewhat shy temperament.

The second born foal was one that was very eagerly awaited. This was the foal of Dolly and Blaze, the two Bell Island ponies. We had been hoping for more females this year, but I wanted Dolly and Blaze's foal to be a male, since

Dolly and Rocky

we needed another stallion of this type. Blaze's owner, Leo, still had a future planned for Blaze as a gelding, so it was important that he have a son who could take his place.

Our wishes were granted. Amid the rocks on the Green's Harbour Winter Sanctuary, Dolly gave birth to a colt at the end of May. Gloria was quickly on the scene, making sure mother and son were all right and putting iodine on the foal's navel to prevent infection. "I think we should call him Rocky," Gloria decided, "since he was born out on the rocks."

Rocky is a big muscular colt growing rapidly on the abundant milk supply from Dolly. What an advertisement for the Bell Island Newfoundland Ponies! He is already a spectacular pony. He has a light brown colour, a white star on his forehead and white rear feet. His musculature is prominent over his body and his legs are thick. With his strong body and strong spirit, Rocky is a good name for him. He will keep the breed alive if he gets half a chance to do so. If he can pass on the great qualities of Dolly and Blaze to a new generation, he will ensure that the old breed he comes from will have a grand future.

Skipper and Blaze had a couple of other foals in the wake of Vicky and Rocky, but all eyes were now on Belle, the mare that had gone to the Black Stallion of Random Island. Belle was in no hurry to deliver, but she eventually foaled in the middle of the night when everyone had given up watching her. Mares like to give birth in secret. Perhaps they inherited this practice from distant ancestors who were the prey of sabre-toothed tigers in pre-historic Europe.

Bill Kennedy, who was caring for Belle, told me, "It was just like last year, when Maggie gave birth to Meg. I'd been watching and waiting to see when it would happen, but then

Belle the mare

I came in early in the morning and there they were, standing up together, Belle and the colt."

It was mid-June and I had come to look at the new foal. He was small, male, with a very dark coat. Bill had decided to name him Blue.

"We all thought he'd be black," I said, "with two black parents."

"It's hard to predict, isn't it?" Bill said. "Of course, their colour often changes as they get older."

"And with Newfoundland Ponies, even the adults change colour with the seasons," I added.

"Well, Blue picked a good time to be born, anyway," said Bill. "Mid-June is the best possible time—winter's over, the spring weather's not so changeable, the sun's giving some warmth and the grass shoots are well up on the pastures."

"Definitely the best time," I agreed. "If they're born too early, there's still the chill of winter in the air, and if they're born late in the season, it's winter again before they've grown enough to cope with it. In a climate like Newfoundland's, foals have to be pretty careful about when they're born!" I chuckled.

A good supply of grass is important so the mares can supply enough milk for the foals. And growing foals can also nibble small amounts of grass and horse feed, which helps them grow faster. Blue was certainly an example of that. He was nibbling grass when he was only a week old and by the time a month had passed, he was getting into his mother's rations. He grew quickly and, although he'd started out small, he was of normal size by his second month.

It was about that time that we decided to have a big round-up of all our Newfoundland Ponies and make one herd of them in a very large pasture in Upper Gullies, Conception Bay. Annie, Dolly, and Belle with their foals would be part of this congregation.

The herd numbered eleven when all the ponies were assembled. The pasture could carry that number of animals. The ages in the group ranged from twenty years down to fifty days. This provided a rich social environment for the three foals. In addition to wise and kind human care, good foals also need horse company in order to become complete individuals. Even the old mares without foals enjoyed the presence of the youngsters.

Bill and I had observed that many of the older ponies we had seen seemed to have hang-ups or personality problems—probably because of poor care or training when they were young. "We don't want any of that in the new generation," I said. "It's important that these foals get the right kind of upbringing if they're going to be the future of their breed."

As we watched the new foals frolicking in their pasture, Bill agreed. "We definitely want the best for our family of foals," he said. "I guess that's what all parents want for their children, isn't it?"

"I think ponies are a lot like kids," I laughed as I watched the two young colts, Rocky and Blue, shoving up against each other while Vicky tried to join in the game. Bringing them all together in a herd, just as ponies had done in the days long ago when they were plentiful all over Newfoundland, would certainly contribute to making them healthy, happy ponies.

"They love to play, don't they?" Bill said. We watched as they broke off one game to begin another, chasing and charging each other around the pasture. It almost seemed as if their games had rules that we humans couldn't understand but the foals knew perfectly well. They would try to push each other down, or mock-fight, biting each other's heads or rearing up face to face with each other. They seemed to have hours of fun.

"They deserve their fun; they've got serious work ahead of them," I said. After all, these playful foals and the others born that year and the year before had to save an isolated branch of a horse family that probably began when the human race began and accompanied mankind, step by step, throughout its history. I couldn't help thinking back on that history as I watched the herd at play.

I tried to imagine those first ponies brought over to Newfoundland in the 1600s, no doubt shaky and nervous after their long sea-voyage, setting uncertain hooves on the soil of their new home. I thought of the many generations of ponies who had worked so hard, pulling ploughs and sled-loads of wood in so many Newfoundland communities in days of old. I remembered the sad neglect that had caused their breed to almost become extinct, and the many kind-hearted people who had cared enough to try to save the Newfoundland Pony.

And I thought back on the ponies I myself had known—right back to Queen, that grand old lady retiring in such dignity. I thought of strong-spirited survivors like Beauty and Whisky who had been neglected and abused but still survived, of hard-working geldings like Prince who had been renamed Cloudy, and the other Prince who had been such a good companion for old Esau. And I thought of the spirited stallions and fine mares who had made this new generation of foals possible. Every one of them—past, present, and future—had a role to play in keeping their breed alive. Whether as pets, workers, or recreational partners, Newfoundland Ponies have shown us what they can still add to our lives, to our environment, and to our province.